Tales From The Caribbean

Traditional tales, fables and sagas

from the Caribbean.

Compiled, Adapted & Edited by Clive Gilson

Tales from the World's Firesides

Part 11 of the series: The Caribbean

Tales From The Caribbean,

edited by Clive Gilson, Solitude, Bath, UK

www.clivegilson.com

First print edition © 2025, Clive Gilson

Printed by IngramSpark

ISBN: 978-1-915081-42-1

- I have edited Clive Gilson's books for over a decade now – he's prolific and can turn his hand to many genres. poetry, short fiction, contemporary novels, folklore, and science fiction – and the common theme is that none of them ever fails to take my breath away. There's something in each story that is either memorably poignant, hauntingly unnerving, or sidesplittingly funny - *Lorna Howarth, The Write Factor*

- *Ragged A**** Ruffian reviewed on Amazon in the United Kingdom on 27 January 2021* - A truly heartwarming, interesting, story with a wonderful narrative. Unquestionably a splendid read

- A Solitude of Stars: With deft turns of phrase and an imagination that would make Philip K. Dick jealous, Gilson foresees a dystopian future, the seeds of which are definitely being sown right now. The story is a chilling glimpse of what may come to pass, warmed by a thread of love that raises the narrative beyond despair. I found the stories disturbing and breath-taking in equal measure. The Apparat and Dirigiste tribes are ranging across our solar system seeking peace by waging war, raising the question; is humanity actually capable of peace? A riveting read. - *Rob Swan, The Write Factor*

- Songs of Bliss gripped me from the start - I had to read right to the end. Loved the humour. Impressed by the surprising empathy that I felt for rather - on the face of it - unlikeable characters. Look forward to seeing it in print. - *Maighdean-Mhara, commenting on Authonomy*

- I just wanted to thank you once more for your help acquiring this beautiful collection. It's found a new home at the top of my library. I've already stumbled onto some wonderful stories in a couple of the collections, and I can't wait to get more. Have a wonderful holiday and a great new year... - *Richer Daniel Laporte, California, December 2021*

Interior image: OpenClipart-Vectors from Pixabay

Cover image: by Clive Gilson

CONTENTS

Preface

I've been collecting and telling stories for a couple of decades now, having had several of my own fictional works published in recent years. My particular focus is on short story writing in the realms of magical realities and science fiction fantasies.

I've always drawn heavily on traditional folk and fairy tales, and in so doing have amassed a digital collection of many thousands of these tales from around the world. It has been one of my long-standing ambitions to gather these stories together and to create a library of tales that tell the stories of places and peoples from all corners of our world.

This collection, *Tales from the Caribbean*, brings together myths, legends, and folktales from across the many islands and coasts that make up this vibrant and culturally complex region. From the rainforests of Dominica to the mangrove swamps of Jamaica, from the bustling port cities of Trinidad to the shadowed hills of Haiti and Cuba, the Caribbean is a place where stories have long walked hand-in-hand with memory, resistance, and magic.

One of my main motivations in undertaking this project has been to preserve and share stories that might otherwise be lost, especially among English-speaking audiences who may not have encountered them before. Many of these tales come from early collectors, often missionaries, colonial officials, or European ethnographers, whose accounts, while valuable, are shaped by the biases and assumptions of their time. The sources I draw from date mainly from the late eighteenth through early twentieth centuries, and as such, reflect a worldview that frequently misrepresented or misunderstood the cultures it was documenting.

In adapting these tales for a contemporary reader, I aim to retain the spirit and power of the original stories, while carefully updating the language and narrative framing with cultural sensitivity. This means acknowledging the troubling perspectives on race, gender, and spirituality that often appear in older sources, without erasing the stories themselves or the people who told them. Where possible, I have added cultural context and attributions.

Importantly, I do not claim ownership or interpretation of these stories. Rather, my role is that of a collector, a curator, and a careful re-teller, honouring the memory of those who told these stories long before they were ever written down. I understand that many of the early collectors, whether intentionally or not, distorted or appropriated the oral traditions they recorded. My aim is not to add to that harm, but to offer these tales respectfully, with full attribution to the original collectors and sources, including the names of their publications, translators, and any editorial notes or context I can provide.

The Caribbean is not one culture, or one tradition. It is a mosaic of Indigenous heritage, African roots, European colonialism, and the countless layers in between. Its stories reflect this rich and often painful history. You'll find trickster tales full of wit and survival; ghost stories that whisper of slavery and sorrow; creation myths that recall rivers, mountains, and stars; and stories of gods and spirits who have crossed oceans alongside the people who once worshipped them.

Throughout the Caribbean, syncretism plays a powerful role, where African Orishas may wear the faces of Catholic saints, and where a French colonial tale might blend with West African storytelling forms. This fusion is not confusion, but rather a symbol of resilience and cultural adaptation, born out of centuries of forced migration, enslavement, and spiritual endurance. These tales are part of the oral legacy of people who have held onto story as a way of remembering, resisting, and remaking the world around them.

Each island, each territory, each community across the Caribbean archipelago brings its own voice to this collection. From Jamaican Anansi stories that travelled from the Ashanti Empire to the sugar plantations, to Haitian legends shaped by Vodou cosmology and revolutionary history, to Lucian Jumbie tales, Trinidadian folklore, Cuban myths, and Dominican mountain spirits, these stories offer insight into not just cultural heritage, but into how people have navigated survival, identity, and imagination across generations.

In this collection, I hope you'll find not only entertainment, but also a deeper connection to the voices and traditions that have helped shape the Caribbean's vibrant cultural landscape. These stories are more than just tales; they are echoes, of laughter and grief, resistance and hope, woven into the very roots of Caribbean soil.

Every effort has been made to accurately credit the original sources, including the early collectors and the titles in which these tales were first published. Notes have been added where possible to give further cultural, historical, or regional context. Where stories are anonymous, or part of oral traditions without a clear author, I have acknowledged their likely cultural origin. In doing so, I hope to honour the people and communities that have kept these tales alive, often in the face of colonial erasure and historical violence.

As for the fireside project, these collections will grow over coming years to tell lost and forgotten tales from every continent, and even then, I'll just be scratching the surface of the world's lore and love. That's the great gift in storytelling. Since the first of our ancestors sat around in a cave, contemplating an ape's place in the world, we have, as a species, continued to tell each other stories of magic and cunning and caution and love. All those years ago, when I began to read through tales from the Celts, tales from Indonesia, tales from Africa and the Far East, tales from everywhere, one of the things that struck me clearly was just how similar are our roots. We share characters and characteristics. The nature of these tales is so similar underneath the local camouflage. Human beings clearly share a storytelling heritage so much deeper than the world that we see superficially as always having been just as it is now.

These tales were originally told by firelight as a way of preserving histories and educating both adult and child. These tales form part of our shared heritage, witches, warts, fantastic beasts, and all. They can be dark and violent. They can be sweet and loving. They are we and we are they in so many ways. I've loved reading and re-reading these stories. I hope that you do too.

Clive

Bath 2025

A Jaguar Who Turned Into A Woman

This story has been adapted from an original tale in Herman van Cappelle Jr's book, Myths and legends from the West Indies, published by Zutphen, Wj Thieme & Cie, in 1926. These tales were originally published in the Dutch language.

Long ago, on an island where the hills rolled green like the backs of sleeping turtles and the sea sang lullabies to the wind, there lived a hunter named Kael. He was not the strongest man in the village, nor the fastest, but when it came to hunting piengos, the wild forest pigs that roamed in clever, chattering bands, there was no one like him.

Kael would return from the forest with five, sometimes six piengos slung over his shoulders, while other hunters, proud and seasoned, came back with one or two, if any at all. Even the jaguar, the silent stalker of the bush, who had hunted piengos since the beginning of time, caught fewer than Kael. The forest murmured about it. The trees, the wind, even the animals watched Kael and wondered: how did he do it?

The jaguar, fierce and ancient, took particular notice. She had prowled the hills and hollows for centuries, queen of the shadows, and no man had bested her, until now. So one evening, when the moon rose full over the canopies and painted the world in silver, she stepped into a clearing and, with a whisper of magic older than language, shed her fur and fangs and took the form of a beautiful woman.

She waited on the forest path until Kael appeared, his hands stained with the hunt, his eyes bright with quiet pride. She greeted him with the softness of mist and said, "You are mighty with the bow, hunter. Tell me, how do you catch so many piengos, when even the jaguar cannot?"

Kael, startled by her beauty and the oddness of her question, simply shrugged. "I have hunted since I was a boy. It's all I've ever known."

She tilted her head, and her eyes glowed amber in the moonlight. "Then let me live beside you. Let me cook your kill and walk the forest at your side. Together, we will bring down even more than before."

Kael was wary. He had heard stories of spirits who wore the skin of women and lured men into the bush, never to be seen again. But her smile was warm, and her words gentle. And so, with a nod that sealed more than he knew, he agreed.

They lived together in a small hut woven from palm and cane, and never was a man more content. The woman, he called her Amara, was a wonder. She cooked like no one he'd known, her cassava and roasted meat so fine they made the elders hum with delight. She could hunt, too, slipping through the bush like smoke, her bow always sure.

One day, as the sun sank low and the sky blushed like a hibiscus flower, Amara asked Kael, "Do you have no mother or father?"

"I do," Kael said. "They live far east, near the river bend."

"Then we must visit," said Amara firmly. "They will think you have vanished."

Kael hesitated, but agreed. "Very well. But let's hunt first, to bring them gifts."

So they hunted together, filling their packs with meat. Then they set off, walking hand in hand beneath the rustling trees until they came to Kael's parents' hut. His mother cried with joy and clasped him tight. But when she saw Amara, she gasped.

"Who is this woman?" she asked.

"I found her in the forest," Kael replied, "and she found me."

The family welcomed her, and for a time all was well. But the villagers were suspicious. Amara was too beautiful, too quiet, too clever in the hunt. And those amber eyes, like fire caught in honey. They began to ask questions. "Where did she come from?" "What is she, truly?"

Kael said nothing.

But his mother grew anxious. One night, while Amara slept, she pressed her son until, heart heavy, he confessed. "She is not truly a woman, Mother. She is a jaguar, born of claw and fang, changed by magic into this shape. But she is kind, and she is mine."

His mother promised to keep the secret. Yet secrets are fragile things, especially where rum flows like rivers and tongues are loosened with cassiri, the strong, sour drink of the islands.

At a village gathering, under a moon swollen with mischief, Kael's mother was coaxed into drinking more than she should. The people laughed, played drums, passed calabash bowls, and when the question came again, "Who is the woman with your son?", she giggled and whispered the truth.

"She's a jaguar," she slurred. "My beautiful daughter-in-law is a beast of the forest."

Amara heard this. She was sitting by the fire, humming a song from a land older than time. Her humming stopped. Her golden eyes darkened. And with a low growl that turned blood to ice, she stood, walked into the forest, and vanished.

Kael chased after her, calling her name. "Amara! Come back! I do not care what they say!" But only the trees answered, rustling in sorrow.

He returned to his mother, heartbroken. "You promised," he said.

"They made me drink," she whispered, tears wetting her cheeks. "I didn't mean to speak."

But the damage was done. From that day forward, Kael never entered the forest without calling her name. He would sit beneath the tallest ceiba tree and wait, whispering, "Amara, my love, my jaguar, come back."

But the forest had swallowed her whole.

And though some say they have seen her shadow in the trees, sleek and silent, watching with eyes of fire, she never returned.

Yet when the piengos run restless through the bush, when the pigs cry out in fear with no hunter near, the old ones say it is her, Amara, the jaguar who once loved a man, now forever wild.

And they say, if you ever meet a beautiful woman in the forest, with amber eyes and a quiet smile, you must never ask where she came from. Just take her hand, and say thank you. Then leave, and never, ever speak her name aloud.

Tiger's Breakfast

This story has been adapted from an original tale in Martha Warren Beckwith's book, Jamaica Anansi Stories, published by The American Folk-Lore Society, New York, in 1924. This story is as told by Richard Morgan, Santa Cruz Mountains..

Once, in the lush hills where the morning mist hung thick over the trees, and the parrots chattered like gossiping neighbours, there lived a clever spider named Anansi. Though small in size, he was known far and wide for his sharp wit, slippery tongue, and unmatched appetite.

Now, Tiger, large, fierce, and proud, lived just down the riverbank. He was a creature of strength and habit, and each morning, without fail, he prepared a rich and hearty breakfast of roasted breadfruit, salted fish, sweet yam mash, and wild honey fresh from the hives. The scent alone was enough to make your stomach turn somersaults.

Anansi, ever the opportunist, made it his business to arrive at Tiger's house each morning just as breakfast was being served.

"Brother Tiger," Anansi would say, puffing out his chest as if he'd just happened by, "your breakfast smells sweeter than a Sunday blessing!"

Tiger, good-natured and not the brightest of beasts, always invited Anansi in to share. And share he did, though Anansi, by some miracle of charm, always seemed to eat twice as much as Tiger himself. But after a week of this, Tiger grew curious.

"Brother Anansi," he said, licking honey from his paws, "you've been enjoying my breakfast plenty lately. When will you return the favour and host me at your home?"

Anansi grinned, his eight eyes glinting with mischief. "Ah, Brother Tiger, tomorrow's the day! But listen carefully. When you arrive, if you hear noise, plates clinking, me humming, or calling out, then come straight in, because breakfast is on. But if all is silent, it means… I'm not ready. You mustn't come in then."

Tiger nodded, none the wiser.

The next morning, Tiger arrived at Anansi's crooked little house on the edge of the bush. He stopped to listen. Not a sound. "Hmm," he thought, "quiet. Best not go in."

But inside, Anansi was already halfway through his meal, smacking his lips, licking the bowls clean, and chuckling to himself.

Later, Tiger returned. "Brother Anansi! I heard nothing. Did I miss breakfast?"

Anansi nodded solemnly. "Ah, Brother Tiger, you know how it is. When a man's eating properly, he can't be making noise, now can he? All that chewing and swallowing… takes concentration."

Tiger scratched his head but didn't argue.

"Don't worry," Anansi added quickly. "Come back tomorrow. And this time, I'll teach you a little breakfast song. When I say 'Nyammy nyammy nyammy', you say 'Nyam is what I eat!' That way, you'll know when to join me."

The next day, Tiger came again. Inside, Anansi was singing, "Nyammy nyammy nyammy!"

Tiger, standing outside, shouted happily, "Nyam is what I eat!"

But Anansi didn't let him in.

"Oh, dear," he muttered through a mouthful of roasted plantain. "Poor Tiger's timing is all off."

Again, Tiger got nothing. Again, Anansi ate enough for two. But Tiger was no fool, at least, not forever. He began to suspect his friend's trickery and resolved to play his own game.

The following day, Anansi returned to Tiger's home. As usual, Tiger laid out a fine breakfast. But this time, as Anansi filled his plate greedily, he asked, "Brother Tiger, where do you find such fine meat every morning? Your table's always full!"

Tiger leaned in, his voice low and serious. "It's no ordinary trick, my friend. When I see a cow resting on the hillside, I sneak up and slip my paw into its belly and pull out the tripe. That way, I always have meat!"

Anansi's eyes widened. He could almost taste the rich stew he'd make. "You don't say!"

He left quickly, already plotting. That very evening, he crept up the hillside where a plump cow lay dozing in the grass. Anansi tiptoed up, humming to himself, and, with great effort, pushed one spindly leg into the cow's belly. But the moment he did, the cow awoke with a snort. Startled, the beast bolted down the hill, dragging poor Anansi behind, his leg stuck fast!

"Brother Cow! Please, don't shut me in! Let me out, nuh!" he cried, but the cow only galloped faster, crashing through bushes and bouncing over rocks, dragging Anansi through mud, briars, and creek water. By the time he was flung loose, bruised, battered, and dizzy, the sun was already high in the sky. He lay flat on his back, staring at the clouds, groaning.

And from that day on, Anansi's belly, once dark and round, was pale and scraped white from all the stones and gravel he'd been dragged across. That, they say, is why Anansi the spider has a white patch on his belly to this very day. So the next time someone tries to cheat you out of breakfast, remember: every trickster gets their turn.

Anansi and Brother Tiger

This story has been adapted from an original tale in Walter Jekyll's book, Jamaican Song And Story, published by David Nutt, London,, in 1907.

One day, Anansi and Brother Tiger went down to the river to bathe. Anansi turned to Brother Tiger and said, "Brother Tiger, you're such a big man, if you go into the deep blue pool with all that fat on you, you're bound to drown! You'd best take your fat off and leave it here on the riverbank."

Brother Tiger replied, "Well then, you should take off yours as well."

Anansi said, "Alright. But you go first, and I'll take mine off after."

So Brother Tiger took off his fat and placed it safely on the bank.

Anansi grinned and said, "Go on then, Brother Tiger, jump into the water so I can see how light you swim without your fat!"

Brother Tiger dived in, and while he was busy splashing about, Anansi crept over to the riverbank, snatched up Tiger's fat, and gobbled it all up.

As soon as he finished, Anansi grew frightened. "Oh no," he thought, "when Tiger finds out, he'll tear me to pieces!" So he ran off from the riverside and made his way to Big Monkey Town. When he got there, he said to the monkeys, "Brothers, I heard a strange little song being sung by the river. It went like this…"

And he began to sing:

"Yesterday this time, I was eating Tiger's fat.

Yesterday this time, I was eating Tiger's fat."

But the big monkeys were not impressed. They waved him away and said, "We don't want to hear any foolish songs like that!"

So off Anansi went again, this time to Little Monkey Town. There, he greeted the monkeys and said, "Brothers, I heard a sweet little tune being sung down by the river. It went like this…"

"Yesterday this time, I was eating Tiger's fat."

The little monkeys were delighted. "Oh, what a brilliant song! Sing it again!"

So Anansi sang the tune over and over. The little monkeys loved it so much that they threw a party that very night and danced to the song until dawn.

When Anansi heard the music playing and his song being sung all through the night, he grinned with delight and said to himself, "Time to see what Brother Tiger's up to…"

So he returned to the river and found Brother Tiger searching frantically by the water.

"Brother Anansi," said Tiger, "I can't find my fat anywhere!"

Anansi chuckled and said, "Ha! Funny thing, I heard an odd song being sung in Little Monkey Town. It went like this…""

"Yesterday this time, I was eating Tiger's fat."

"If you think I'm lying, come with me and see for yourself."

So the two of them went to Little Monkey Town. When they arrived, Anansi told Tiger to hide with him in the bushes just outside the village. And what did they hear? The monkeys were dancing and singing the same tune loud and proud:

"Yesterday this time, I was eating Tiger's fat.

Yesterday this time, I was eating Tiger's fat."

"Brother Tiger," said Anansi, "Didn't I tell you? You hear them singing your name in that song?"

Tiger couldn't take it anymore. He marched straight into the monkey's party and shouted, "Where's my fat? I want it back!"

The monkeys looked at him, confused. "We don't know anything about your fat," they said. "Mr Anansi's the one who taught us that song!"

Tiger turned to Anansi, furious. Then he lunged at the little monkeys, ready for a fight., but the little monkeys weren't alone. They quickly sent a message to Big Monkey Town, and before long, an army of monkey soldiers arrived. Together, they gave Brother Tiger and Anansi a proper beating.

Tiger had no choice but to flee into the forest, and Anansi ran up to the rooftop of the nearest house to hide. And from that day on, Tiger has lived in the bush, and Anansi has lived on rooftops, each one keeping far away from the other, each remembering the song that started it all.

"Yesterday this time, I was eating Tiger's fat."

The Boat of Phantom Children

This story has been adapted from an original tale in Charles M. Skinner's book, Myths & Legends of our New Possessions & Protectorate, published by J. B. Lippincott Company, Philadelphia & London, 1900.

Long ago, when the Caribbean was a battleground of empires, when great ships clashed on the waves and the cries of war echoed over the turquoise waters, there lived a man feared by all who called these islands home. He was Sir Francis Drake, also known as the Dragon, the scourge of the Spanish Main, a man whose name was whispered in dread among the colonists and the enslaved alike. He brought fire and steel wherever he sailed, and though his victories were many, his sins were greater still.

One December, near the coast of what is now Colombia, Drake and his fleet came upon a small Spanish village nestled near Rio de la Hacha. The people, knowing well the destruction he would bring, fled. They buried their few treasures beneath the sand, abandoned their homes, and hurriedly loaded their families into boats, hoping to reach the safety of a distant cape before the English fleet could strike. But in their rush, they could not take everyone.

A single fishing smack was left behind, carrying fifty of the village's children. The boat was entrusted to an old fisherman, whose weathered hands had guided it across those waters for years. As the storm clouds gathered on the horizon, he hoisted the sails and steered toward the meeting point where the others would wait for them.

But fate was cruel. Before the smack could reach safety, Drake's fleet arrived. The English galleons surged toward the shore, their cannons glinting in the light of the coming storm. Seeing the lone vessel bobbing on the waves, Drake assumed it was a scout or a supply ship for the Spanish forces. He gave the order. The cannons thundered.

Two great shots tore through the air, their sound splitting the heavens. The fisherman cried out as the force of the cannon fire sent his small boat veering wildly into the raging sea. The last thing the villagers saw before the storm swallowed it was their children, clutching each other, calling out for their parents, their voices lost in the howling wind.

The smack never returned.

The next morning, after the storm had passed and the English fleet had gone, the villagers crept back from their hiding place, grief and rage burning in their hearts. They scanned the sea, praying for a miracle, for some sign that their children had survived.

And then, they saw it. A boat appeared in the distance, rocking gently on the waves. The people ran to the pier, their cries of joy rising like the dawn itself.

As it drew closer, they saw their children standing aboard, smiling, laughing, reaching out. Their small hands beckoned, and their eyes gleamed like sunlight on the water. But as the boat neared the shore, something was clearly wrong. The children's forms began to waver, as if they were no longer solid. Their bright faces drooped, their limbs hung limp, and their voices faded to whispers. The outline of the boat blurred, melting into mist before their eyes. And then, it was gone.

The villagers wailed in grief, and their cries became curses upon Drake's name. They swore that he would never know peace, that the sea itself would carry the spirits of their lost ones to torment him. And so it did.

Not long after, Drake's fleet was beset by unnatural storms. Everywhere he sailed, the ghostly smack followed. Before each tempest, before each misfortune, the phantom vessel would appear, its spectral children standing silently upon its deck, their hollow eyes fixed upon him.

The once-fearless commander became haunted, his strength drained by fever, his heart darkened by remorse. No victory could lift his spirits. No plunder could fill the abyss that had formed within him. The Boat of Phantom Children had marked him.

In January, his body could take no more. Suffering from an unknown sickness, he lay dying aboard his ship off the coast of Nombre de Dios. In his final moments, he saw the vision once more, the boat rising from the mist, the children staring, silent and still.

And as his body was lowered into the sea, the crew, looking back over the dark waves, saw it one last time.

The phantom boat emerged from the deep, its sails billowing with no wind, its small figures gazing toward the place where Drake's body had sunk. Then, just as suddenly, it turned toward the shore and vanished into the morning mist.

To this day, sailors claim that on stormy nights, near the coasts of Colombia and beyond, you can see it, the Boat of Phantom Children, forever searching, forever haunting, its ghostly crew waiting to claim the next soul who dares to forget the price of cruelty upon the sea.

The Origin Of The First Humans

This story has been adapted from an original tale in Herman van Cappelle Jr's book, Myths and legends from the West Indies, published by Zutphen—Wj Thieme & Cie, in 1926. These tales were originally published in the Dutch language.

Long ago, before the islands were kissed by the waves and the winds, the People of the Sky lived in a world of light and laughter. They had everything they needed, golden fruits that never withered, rivers of sweet water, and the songs of the stars to guide their dreams. But among them were the Curious Ones, those who longed to know what lay beyond their perfect sky.

One day, as they wandered near the edge of their shining world, they found a crack in the sky's fabric. Peering through, they gasped in wonder. Below them stretched another world, one covered in emerald forests, silver rivers, and a golden sun that burned brighter than their own.

They had to see it for themselves. So they braided long ropes of bast fibres, strong and supple, and let them hang through the crack. One by one, the Curious Ones climbed down, their feet touching the earth for the first time. They ran through the forests, felt the coolness of the rivers, and danced beneath the sun. The world was wild, untamed, and full of new wonders.

But after a time, they grew homesick. They missed the sky, the fruits that never withered, and the comfort of the songs they had always known. So they gathered together beneath the crack in the heavens and began to climb back up.

One by one, they ascended, until the last of them, a woman whose body was broad and heavy, tried to follow. As she squeezed through the opening, she became stuck. No one could push her up, nor could she pull herself free. The others, still below, grew impatient. They pulled and pushed, but in the struggle, the rope of bast fibres snapped, and the last of the Curious Ones plummeted to earth. They were trapped.

At first, they did not despair. They searched for food, believing this world would provide for them as the sky had done. But the fruits were bitter, the rivers empty of sweetness. Nothing tasted as it should. With no other choice, they ate the soil itself, shaping it into cakes and drying them in the sun. They ate, and they ate, but still, they grew thinner. Their bones ached, their bellies growled, and the world that had once seemed so full of promise now felt like a prison of hunger.

But they noticed something strange. Though they withered, the Acouri, the swift little rodent of the jungle, grew fat and strong. It must have found something better to eat. The People of the Sky had to know its secret.

First, they sent the Woodpecker to watch. But the foolish bird tapped against the tree trunks, betraying its presence, and the Acouri fled.

Then, they sent the Alligator, thinking it would be clever and silent. But the Alligator, thinking only of itself, returned with a lie, claiming it had seen nothing. Enraged, the People punished it, cutting out its tongue so it would never again speak falsehoods. Finally, they sent the Rat. But the Rat, greedy for what it had found, never returned. And so, the People of the Sky wasted away.

In their despair, they left the place of their fall, wandering elsewhere in search of food. They abandoned all but one, a single child, too small to survive the journey. But when the people returned, many moons later, expecting to find nothing but bones, they were astonished. The child was alive. More than that, the child was healthy, its belly round with good food. Surrounding it were golden stalks, taller than a man, with ears of grain bursting from their tops.

The Acouri had cared for the child, feeding it the golden kernels from the stalks. The child, in turn, had followed the Acouri and discovered its secret, the first cornfield. The People of the Sky rejoiced, for they knew they had been saved. They learned to harvest the corn, to plant it in the earth, and to call upon the spirits of the rain and the sun to nourish it. And so, they grew in number.

Though they never returned to the heavens, they built their homes beneath the stars, remembering always that they had once come from another world. And when they looked up at the sky, they saw the crack, still glimmering faintly, and knew that one day, when their time was done, they would find their way back home.

And so, the People of the Sky became the first People of the Earth. And from them, all the children of the Caribbean were born.

Yung-Kyum-Pyung

This story has been adapted from an original tale in Walter Jekyll's book, Jamaican Song And Story, published by David Nutt, London,, in 1907.

Once upon a time, there was a king who had three daughters, but no one in the whole world knew their names. All the wisest scholars, magicians, and noblemen came from far and wide to guess them, but not a single soul could figure them out.

Now, when Brother Anansi heard about this, he said to himself, "Me? I'm the one who'll find out their names. Not a man alive can manage it, but me? Of course I can."

So, one day, the king's three daughters went out to bathe in the river. Anansi, being the trickster he was, made a beautiful little basket, so lovely that anyone who saw it would want to shout. He left the basket in a room where he knew the princesses would come later to eat their meal. Then, clever as ever, he crept underneath the house and waited quietly, listening.

Before long, the girls returned. And as soon as they saw the basket, they were completely enchanted. It was the most beautiful thing they had ever seen.

The eldest daughter exclaimed, "Yung-kyum-pyung! What a gorgeous basket! Margaret-Powell-Alone! What a beautiful basket!"

Then the second daughter chimed in, "Margaret-Powell-Alone! Look at this lovely basket! Eggie-Law! I've never seen one so fine!"

And the youngest burst out, laughing with delight, saying, "Eggie-Law! What a basket, eh? Yung-kyum-pyung! Just look at it!"

Anansi, hiding under the floorboards, heard every word. His eyes gleamed with mischief, and he smiled so wide you'd think his head would split. Without making a sound, he crept away.

Not long after, he put together a band, with drums and fiddles, and taught the musicians a special tune that included the names of the three daughters.

After a week had passed, Anansi returned to the palace. Once he was close enough for the King to hear, he shouted, "Strike up the music! Let's play!"

The band began to play and sing, loud and joyful:

Yung-kyum-pyung!

Eggie-Law!

Margaret-Powell-Alone!

They sang it again and again, letting the names echo across the palace courtyard.

The Queen heard it first. "Who's that shouting out my daughters' names?" she cried.

Anansi waved for the band to play louder.

The Queen, in such a fluster, came rushing down the stairs, tripped, and broke her neck on the way.

Still the music played.

Yung-kyum-pyung!

Eggie-Law!

Margaret-Powell-Alone!

Then the King heard the racket and roared from his throne, "Who dares to call out the names of my daughters?"

The band played louder still, singing the tune over and over.

Finally, the King was so shocked that he threw himself off his throne, and dropped dead right there on the palace floor.

And that was the end of that.

Anansi, ever the trickster, climbed the steps to the empty throne, married the youngest daughter, and declared himself ruler of the kingdom.

Now, they say Anansi was the wickedest king who ever ruled. Some days he was there. Some days he'd vanish, off running on his web of ropes, stealing cows for his wife. And that's how Brother Anansi became king, by trick, by tune, and a bit of trouble.

Day-Time Trouble – Rabbit And Anansi

This story has been adapted from an original tale in Martha Warren Beckwith's book, Jamaica Anansi Stories, published by The American Folk-Lore Society, New York, in 1924. This story is as told by Vivian Bailey, Mandeville.

It was a bright, hot day in the hills of St. Ann, and the world shimmered with the heavy quiet of noon. The sun hung high in the sky like a lazy lantern, and the trees rustled softly in the breeze. Out from the bushes came two figures, Brother Anansi, the spider trickster, all legs and mischief, and his companion Brother Rabbit, curious and unsuspecting as ever.

They were strolling together, as friends sometimes do when there's nothing in particular to do and nowhere urgent to be. As they walked, Rabbit turned to Anansi with a little laugh.

"Brother Anansi," he said, "you always talking 'bout 'daytime trouble'. But me never see what that is. Show me nah? Just once. I want to know what all the fuss is about."

Anansi gave a dry chuckle, as though he found the idea amusing, or foolish. "You sure?" he asked, peering sideways at Rabbit. "You sure you want to see 'daytime trouble'? It's not play-play business, you know."

Rabbit, ever confident and a little too eager, puffed out his chest. "Man like me? I can handle anything."

"Alright then," said Anansi, eyes gleaming. "You've asked for it."

They walked a little further until, ahead of them in a small clearing, Anansi spotted something rare and dangerous. It was Tiger, resting beneath a mango tree, surrounded by his cubs.

Without a word of warning, Anansi tiptoed over, snatched one of the young tigers, and, quick as lightning, killed it.

Rabbit gasped in horror. "What are you doing?! Are you mad?!"

"Shh," Anansi hissed. He sliced a piece of meat from the cub, dropped it into a basket, and handed it to Rabbit. "Here," he said. "Go give this to Tiger. Tell him it's a gift, from you."

Rabbit's eyes widened. "What?! You want me dead?!"

But Anansi was already heading toward Tiger's house, dragging poor Rabbit along behind him. When they arrived, Anansi stepped back and pushed Rabbit forward. "Go on, Brother Rabbit. Hand him the basket."

Trembling, Rabbit did as he was told. He held the basket out to Tiger, who looked inside, saw the flesh of his own child, and let out a roar so loud it shook the trees. With a wild yell, Tiger lunged. But Rabbit, though scared out of his wits, bolted, while Anansi, already halfway up a nearby tree, shouted down, "Run, Brother Rabbit, RUN! Run to the stone-hole!"

As Rabbit darted across the field, Anansi tossed him something sharp and shiny. It was a razor. "Take this!" he cried. "You'll need it!"

Rabbit dove into a hollow beneath a large stone, just seconds before Tiger's claws could swipe his tail. Safe, for now, in the dark, narrow hole, he listened as the world above filled with angry voices. Tiger had gathered a search party, a crowd of beasts, furious and ready for revenge.

"He must come out!" Tiger shouted. "Drag him out if you must!"

But none of them could reach him. The hole was too deep and too narrow.

"Send for Reindeer!" someone cried. "Reindeer has got a long neck. He can reach down and drag him out!"

So Reindeer was summoned, his great antlers catching the sun as he approached. He bent low, poking his head into the hole, calling sweetly. "Brother Rabbit, come out now. No one is going to hurt you. We just want a little word."

But Rabbit remembered Anansi's warning. And the razor still gleamed in his paws. The moment Reindeer's head was deep inside, Rabbit struck. One quick, clean slice. Off came Reindeer's head. The crowd above screamed. The body collapsed. There was panic, pure chaos. The animals scattered, shouting and tripping over one another, afraid that some new magic was at work. No one had expected that.

When silence returned to the clearing, Rabbit slowly crawled out, blinking in the sunlight. Anansi was sitting in a tree branch, legs swinging lazily. "Well then," said Anansi with a grin, "now you see. That's what daytime trouble looks like."

Rabbit, still shaking, could only nod.

"And remember," Anansi continued, "you asked for it. So let that be a lesson. As long as you live, never ask anyone to show you daytime trouble again."

And from that day forward, Brother Rabbit never did.

The Serpent's Curse

This story has been adapted from an original tale in L. Roy Terwilliger's book, Cuban Folk-Lore, published by Avisador Comercial Printing House, Havana in 1908. This is a Cuban tale.

Long ago, during the great Ten Years' War in Cuba, when even the wealthiest families found themselves facing hardship, there lived a man named Don Ernesto. He had once been a prosperous landowner, but the tides of revolution had stripped many of his riches, leaving him to manage his estate with dwindling resources. Still, he held on to his pride and his resentment toward those who relied on him.

Among those who sought his help was his own father, Don Rafael, an old man with trembling hands and tired eyes. Each day, when the sun was high in the sky and the scent of simmering stew drifted from the kitchen, Don Rafael would arrive at his son's hacienda, hoping for a warm meal and the comfort of family. Don Ernesto's resources had dwindled, and so had his generosity, and he began to see his father's visits as a burden rather than a blessing.

One day, as hunger gnawed at his household and frustration simmered in his heart, Don Ernesto devised a cruel plan. As noon approached and the familiar sound of his father's cane tapping against the cobbled path reached the door, he turned to his wife and servants and said, "Today, we do not eat until he leaves."

The meal was hidden away, the table left bare. When Don Rafael stepped inside, he glanced around, his brow furrowing.

"Has the meal already been served?" he asked, his voice lined with weariness.

Don Ernesto, without meeting his father's eyes, nodded. "Yes, Papá, we ate early today."

A shadow of disappointment crossed the old man's face, but he said nothing. He gripped his cane tighter, nodded stiffly, and turned away. The door shut behind him with a finality that made even the servants shift uneasily. But Don Ernesto felt no regret.

With his father gone, he clapped his hands. "Now, bring the food at once! We've waited long enough."

The servants hurried to the kitchen, lifting the heavy kettle that had been left to simmer over the fire. But something was wrong. The lid would not budge. The cook, a stout woman with strong arms, pulled and pried, but the cover seemed fused to the pot. Panic crept into her eyes as she whispered a hurried prayer.

The master of the house, irritated beyond measure, stormed into the kitchen. "Must I do everything myself?" he snapped, seizing the lid. With a mighty yank, he pulled it free.

Suddenly a monstrous hissing filled the air, and from the bubbling stew, something moved. The thick coils of a serpent, longer than any man, its scales gleaming like molten silver, rose from the pot, steam curling from its glistening body. It unfurled, its forked tongue flickering, its golden eyes locking onto Don Ernesto. A deep, unnatural chill settled over the kitchen. Screams rang through the hacienda as the serpent lunged.

Before Don Ernesto could flee, the beast wrapped itself around him, its powerful coils tightening, pressing against his ribs, forcing the air from his lungs. He clawed at the scales, but they were hard as iron, and utterly unyielding. The more he struggled, the tighter the serpent constricted.

The household erupted in chaos. The servants ran to fetch help, but none dared approach the monstrous creature. The children cried, while his wife fell to her knees, praying for mercy. But there would be none. As Don Ernesto gasped for breath, he understood. This was no ordinary serpent. This was a punishment.

The weight of his sins crashed down upon him. He had turned away his own father, and lied to the man who had given him life, all to hoard a meal that was now cursed beyond reckoning. This was the fates delivering justice.

With the last of his strength, his voice hoarse with terror, he cried, "Señor Milagroso! Papá! I beg you, I will make amends! I vow, before Heaven, to offer a silver image of this moment, so that all may remember the price of my selfishness!"

As the words left his lips, the serpent released him. It slithered from his body, its great length coiling once around the room before sinking into the shadows of the hearth, vanishing as suddenly as it had come.

Don Ernesto collapsed onto the cold stone floor, his chest heaving, his heart racing. He had been spared, but he would never forget the feel of the serpent's coils, in the near-death grip of his own cruelty.

The very next day, he travelled to the nearest town and commissioned a silver sculpture of a serpent coiled around a kneeling man, just as he had promised. He placed it in the village church, where it stood as a warning for generations to come, a tale told by father to son, as a reminder that to turn away family in their time of need was to invite the wrath of the serpent.

And so, in the heart of Cuba, beneath the watchful eyes of saints and candles, the Serpent's Curse has never been forgotten.

The Deluge

This story has been adapted from an original tale in Charles M. Skinner's book, Myths & Legends of our New Possessions & Protectorate, published by J. B. Lippincott Company, Philadelphia & London, 1900.

Long before the arrival of white men with their iron tools and their hunger for gold, the islands of the Caribbean belonged to the great forces of nature and the spirits that moved unseen through the land and sea. The people of the Antilles lived in harmony with these spirits, honouring the waters, the forests, and the sky. But there came a time when the balance was broken, and the ocean itself was unleashed from its bounds.

On an island that would one day be called Hispaniola, there ruled a powerful cacique named Guayacán. He was a man of wisdom and strength, beloved by his people, but troubled by a great sorrow. His eldest son, Yarael, had grown reckless and bold, challenging his father's authority, speaking of power that should belong to the young, not the old. One night, overcome by rage and fear, Guayacán struck down his own son.

Regret filled the chief's heart the moment Yarael's breath left him. The father who had taken life now sought to preserve what was left. He cleaned the bones of his child with care and placed them within a hollowed-out gourd, a vessel once used to store fresh water from the rivers. He and his wife kept the gourd hidden away, and often, when the grief became too great, they would open it to gaze upon what remained of their lost son.

But the gods had seen Guayacan's crime, and they did not forget. One day, when the chief and his warriors had gone deep into the jungle to hunt, his four surviving sons were left behind in the village. They were curious about the gourd their father had placed so reverently atop their home, away from the reach of all others. What could be so precious inside? What power had their father hidden away?

One brother reached for the gourd, cradling it in his hands. Another took it, feeling its weight. They laughed nervously, debating whether they should open it. Surely just a quick look would do no harm. Then, it slipped. The gourd shattered upon the stone floor, its pieces scattering like fallen leaves. But no bones remained inside.

Instead, a rush of water burst forth, as if the gourd had been a dam holding back a great and terrible flood. At first, the brothers laughed, thinking it a trick. But the water did not stop. It rose over their feet, lapping at their ankles. Within moments, it reached their knees. The ground that had been dry only heartbeats before became a rushing river. And from the gourd's remains, creatures began to emerge. Whales. Sharks. Great silver fish. Writhing eels and snapping turtles.

The sea had been imprisoned within the gourd, and now it had been set free.

The brothers ran, climbing the hills as fast as their legs would carry them, but the water was faster. The village was swallowed whole. The forests disappeared beneath the rising waves. The sacred caves, the places where their ancestors had once gathered to tell their stories, were lost to the current.

Still, the water rose. The people who lived on the lowest lands were the first to be taken, their cries drowned beneath the roar of waves. Then the rivers themselves were swallowed, becoming part of the ever-growing sea. The mountains, once towering above all, became the last refuge of those who had not yet been claimed. But the flood did not stop.

Guayacán returned with his warriors to find his home gone, his people scattered, his remaining sons clinging to the highest peaks. He saw what they had done, saw the broken gourd, and understood. This was the punishment of the gods, for his crime of slaying his own son, for attempting to contain what should never have been held.

And so, the floodwaters never receded. The lands that had once stretched far and wide remained beneath the endless blue. What was once the great land of the ancestors had become the islands of the Antilles, the last peaks that had refused to drown. And to this day, the sea is filled with the creatures that were released from the gourd, forever swimming, forever searching for their lost home.

The people of the Caribbean never forgot this tale. They knew that the sea had once been held back, and that it could just as easily rise again. And so, to this day, the elders warn their children; never take more than you need, never tempt the spirits, and never forget that the ocean remembers all things.

The Origin Of The Caribbean

This story has been adapted from an original tale in Herman van Cappelle Jr's book, Myths and legends from the West Indies, published by Zutphen—Wj Thieme & Cie, in 1926. These tales were originally published in the Dutch language.

Long ago, before the islands of the Caribbean had names, and before the waves carried the songs of men, the rivers ran wild and deep, and the spirits of the land and water moved freely between the two worlds. It was in this time that a water camoudi, a great serpent of the river, fell in love with a maiden of the people.

Each night, as the moon spread silver across the water, the camoudi would shed its monstrous form and walk upon the land as a man, tall and strong, with skin dark as the river stones and hair like the reeds that swayed on the banks. The maiden, enchanted by his beauty and the mystery of his presence, met him in secret beneath the great ceiba tree. She never told her father or her brothers where she went, for she knew they would fear the serpent-man and forbid her from returning.

For many moons, they met in this way. When the night was deep, they spoke of their love in hushed tones, their laughter mingling with the rustling of fallen leaves. And when the dawn broke, the camoudi would slip back into the river, his body stretching long and sinuous beneath the current.

One night, the young woman bore a child, a child unlike any seen before. It was neither fully of the land nor fully of the water. It had the soft skin of a human but the gleaming, golden eyes of the serpent. It moved through the river like its father, yet it had limbs like its mother. The young camoudi-child would play upon the sandbanks, gliding through the shallows, darting between the reeds, and then disappearing back into its watery home.

Still, the young woman kept her secret. But secrets do not stay hidden forever.

One evening, as the young woman lingered longer than usual by the river, her father began to wonder. "Where does my daughter go each night?" he asked his sons. "Why does she stay by the water so long?"

The brothers did not know, but curiosity burned within them. So, the next night, they followed her. Silent as jaguars, they crept through the underbrush and peered between the trees. What they saw froze them in place. Their sister stood on the shore, wrapped in the embrace of a monstrous serpent, its great coils gleaming in the moonlight. And near them, playing in the shallows, was a strange young creature, half human, half beast.

The brothers watched in horror as the great serpent brought food for the child, his forked tongue flicking in and out in the night air. At last, they could stand no more. They fled back to their father and told him all that they had seen.

The old man's face darkened. "This is an abomination," he said. "No child of mine will share blood with a beast. You must kill them at once."

At the first light of dawn, the brothers returned to the riverbank with their spears. They waited until dusk, when the great camoudi slithered onto the shore, his golden eyes glowing in the early moon light. Without hesitation, they struck.

The serpent reared back, hissing in fury, his massive coils thrashing. The earth trembled, and the river churned. But the brothers were swift, and together they drove their spears deep into his body. With a final, shuddering sigh, the camoudi fell still.

Their sister, seeing what had been done, screamed in anguish. But the brothers did not stop. They waded into the shallows, grabbed the young camoudi-child, and dragged it into the forest.

"This creature is not our kin," they said.

Deep into the jungle they ran, their prize writhing in their grip. When they reached a hidden grove, they laid the young serpent upon a stone and, with sharp knives, they cut it into pieces. The remains they scattered among the roots of the trees, believing they had erased the last trace of their sister's shame.

Months passed, and the brothers thought no more of their deed. Then, one day while hunting, they heard voices in the wind, low murmurs, rising and falling like the sighing wind in bare branches. Their skin prickled, for no one should have been in that part of the forest.

Following the voices, they came upon a place they did not recognize, but it should have been familiar, for it was the very spot where they had slain the camoudi-child. Yet now, where there had been only trees and vines, there stood four huts. Smoke curled from their roofs, and strange figures moved among them.

As the brothers drew closer, a man emerged from the first hut. He was tall, his skin gleaming like river stone, his eyes bright and golden. He smiled. "Welcome, my uncles," he said.

The brothers' blood turned to ice.

The man continued, "Do you not recognize us? We were born from the child you killed. From each piece of its body, we have risen, and we have made this place our home."

Then, from the other huts, more figures appeared. Their faces were familiar, yet strange, human in form, yet something else lurked beneath their skin. Their golden eyes glowed like fireflies in the dusk.

The brothers saw their mistake too late.

From the second and third huts, the people gripped their weapons and stepped forward with dark intent. "They killed our father," one murmured. "They killed our mother's child. Why should they live?"

The brothers tensed, their hands inching toward their own weapons.

But the eldest of the serpent-men raised his hand. "No," he said firmly. "They are our uncles. They will not be harmed. Blood must not spill between kin."

And so, the brothers were spared.

Trembling, they returned to their father and told him all that they had seen. The old man's eyes grew wide with wonder. "So, my daughter's child has given birth to a people," he mused. "My blood flows through them, even if they are not as we are."

The next morning, the old man and his sons journeyed to the serpent-men's village. When he beheld his new grandchildren, so many and so strong, his heart swelled with pride.

"This must be celebrated," he declared.

And so, they prepared great vats of paiwarri, the sacred drink of the ancestors. For many days and nights, the village feasted, danced, and sang beneath the stars.

Thus, the first people of the Caribbean were born, not from man alone, but from the blood of the river and the spirit of the great camoudi. And to this day, the descendants of the serpent-child walk among us, their golden eyes watching from the shadows, their spirits bound forever to the land and the sea.

How Monkey Managed Anansi

This story has been adapted from an original tale in Walter Jekyll's book, Jamaican Song And Story, published by David Nutt, London,, in 1907.

One day, Mr Anansi and his wife were sitting under a tree, completely unaware that Mr Monkey was up in the branches above, listening to everything they were saying.

Anansi turned to his wife and said, "You know, I could really do with a bit of fresh meat."

His wife looked at him. "What kind of fresh meat?"

"What do you mean, what kind?" said Anansi. "Any meat at all, my dear. Here's what we're going to do. Let's get an empty banana barrel and lay it on the bed, dress it up to look like a man. We'll wrap it from head to toe in a white sheet so it looks like a body. Then you go and call Brother Cow, Brother Monkey, Brother Sheep, Brother Goat, and Brother Hog. Once they arrive, we'll invite them all inside the house, and you'll wait with them in the room."

So Mrs Anansi sent out word, and before long, Brother Sheep, Brother Goat, Brother Hog, and Brother Monkey all arrived. Brother Cow, who also served as the village parson, came as well.

When they reached Anansi's yard, they found him weeping loudly.

"Oh, don't cry so much, my dear friend," said Parson Cow. "Death comes for us all in the end."

"You don't understand, Brother Cow," sniffed Anansi. "That was my father! My one and only father. Brother Cow, as you're the parson, please take the others inside. Go and look at him lying there, poor soul."

Now, while all this was happening, Mrs Anansi was already inside the room, sitting by the 'body'. Reverend Cow moved to lift the sheet to look at the face, but Mrs Anansi quickly stopped him.

"No," she said. "My husband said no one's to look on his father's face until morning."

So Cow left the sheet untouched.

But up in the tree, Monkey had heard everything Anansi and his wife had planned. So when the others were going into the house, Monkey and his wife stayed where they were.

Anansi called out, "Brother Monkey, come inside and say goodbye to the old man."

But Monkey shook his head. "No, Brother Anansi, I feel too sorry for you. If I go in there, I'll just end up crying all night."

"Come on, Brother Monkey," insisted Anansi. "Go in and keep the others company. You're my closest friend!"

But Monkey refused to go. So Anansi gave up on Monkey, for Monkey was far too clever.

By then, Anansi had already sharpened his cutlass and hidden it behind the door. Once everyone was inside, he closed and locked the only door in the house and sat down behind it.

Then he turned to Parson Cow. "Would you say a word of prayer for my poor father?"

As Cow began praying, Anansi started wailing even louder.

Brother Hog, in his deep old voice, said, "Stay strong, Mr Anansi, stay strong."

And Anansi cried all the harder.

When the prayer ended, Anansi asked Cow to lead them in a hymn. Cow started to sing, choosing Hymn Number One Hundred from the book.

Me going home to St John,

Me going home to St John,

I've seen the last today,

I've seen the last, Father's gone.

But as Cow sang, Anansi suddenly jumped up, shouting, "No! No! I don't like that hymn!" In the same breath, he pulled out the cutlass and began swinging wildly. "I told you, I don't like that hymn!"

The poor guests had no weapons and no way out. Anansi had locked the door. He attacked them mercilessly, killing every one of them.

In the morning, when Anansi opened the door, Monkey, who had stayed hidden all along, burst out laughing. "Brother Anansi," he said, "If I'd stepped foot in your house last night, you'd have done the same to me!"

"No, no," said Anansi quickly. "I would never!"

But to calm Monkey and keep him quiet, Anansi handed him a piece of meat from the very friends he'd just killed.

New Names

This story has been adapted from an original tale in Martha Warren Beckwith's book, Jamaica Anansi Stories, published by The American Folk-Lore Society, New York, in 1924. This story is as told by Samuel Christie, St. Ann's Bay..

Once upon a time, in the warm hills just beyond St. Ann's Bay, there lived four unlikely friends, Anansi the Spider, Tiger, Parrot, and Tacoomah. They were not the sort of company you'd expect to find strolling along together, but such was the strange way of things in those days.

One morning, Anansi, who was always up to some clever scheme, gathered his companions beneath a breadfruit tree. "I have a splendid idea," he said, smoothing his many legs with self-importance. "Let's go on a journey, a real journey, over hills and through valleys. But let's make it interesting. We each must choose a brand new name for the journey. No old names allowed!"

The others agreed, though they knew Anansi well enough to be suspicious. There was always a trick hidden somewhere in his ideas, like a pepper in the rice.

Anansi grinned, his eyes glittering. "But there's one more rule. When we return home, we must each visit our mother. If she calls us by our old name… well… we must eat her."

"Eat her?" said Parrot, fluffing his feathers in alarm.

"Those are the rules," said Anansi, feigning sorrow. "Harsh but fair."

Still, the others agreed. Maybe it was the heat of the day, or maybe they simply weren't as clever as they liked to think. They picked their new names:

Anansi became Che-che-bun-da.

Parrot became Green-corn-ero.

Tiger became Yellow-prissenda.

Tacoomah became Tacoomah-vengeance.

And off they went, singing and laughing, each one trying to remember their new, ridiculous names.

When they returned from their journey, the first stop was Tacoomah's house. Anansi, with a sly grin, reminded everyone, "He's not just Tacoomah, he's Tacoomah-vengeance now."

But when they reached the hut, Tacoomah's poor old mother came rushing out. "Tacoomah! My sweet Tacoomah!" she cried, arms wide to embrace her son.

There was a silence.

Then, by the rules of the bargain, Tacoomah was obliged to kill and eat his own mother, and so he did.

Next, they visited Tiger's home.

"Remember," said Anansi, "his name is Yellow-prissenda."

But just like before, Tiger's mother opened her door and beamed with joy. "My Tiger is home!"

And once again, the terrible deed was done.

That night, as the group rested in the hills, Anansi made an excuse to slip away.

"My belly feels uneasy," he lied. "I need to walk it off."

He crept down to his mother's house and knocked gently. "Mum," he said, in a low, urgent whisper, "tomorrow, when we come here, you must not call me Anansi. If you do, the others will eat you. My name is Che-che-bun-da now. Repeat it after me."

His mother, confused but obedient, repeated, "Che-che-bun-da."

Anansi made her repeat it again and again, until she could say it in her sleep.

The next day, the group made their way to Parrot's home. And just as before, his mother greeted him with joy. "Parrot! My sweet Parrot has come!"

And so, as per the agreement, she too was devoured.

That night, Anansi again snuck away to his mother. "Do you remember what I told you?" he whispered.

"Of course," she said. "Your name is Che-che-bun-da."

He smiled. "Say it again."

"Che-che-bun-da."

"Again."

"Che-che-bun-da, Che-che-bun-da, Che-che-bun-da."

Anansi went to bed that night with a full belly and a quiet heart.

The next evening, the four returned to his mother's home. As they approached, they began to sing their travelling song:

"Anansi's name is Che-che-bun-da,

Cherry-senda, Yellow-prissenda.

Parrot's name is Green-corn-ero,

Cherry-senda, Yellow-prissenda.

Tiger's name is Yellow-prissenda,

Cherry-senda, Yellow-prissenda.

Tacoomah's name is Tacoomah-vengeance,

Cherry-senda, Yellow-prissenda!"

Anansi's mother saw them coming and stood tall at the door. "Look!" she cried, loud and proud. "Here comes my son, Che-che-bun-da!"

The others froze. She had said the right name.

Anansi looked at his friends with mock disappointment

The Bacoo

I've collected versions of this tale from various online and paper sources and this story is my own telling of the legend of the Bacoo. The legend of The Bacoo is primarily associated with Guyana, Trinidad and Tobago, and Barbados. However, it is also known in other parts of the Caribbean where African and Indigenous folklore have blended over time.

The waves lapped against the wooden hull of the fishing boat as Saul pulled his net from the sea. He squinted against the early morning sun, sighing at the meagre catch writhing in the tangled mesh. His wife, Celeste, was expecting their second child, and with the poor fish harvests of late, he feared they would struggle to feed their growing family.

As he tossed the last of his haul into the basket, something in the water caught his eye. Bobbing gently against the current was a small, corked bottle, its glass green and dulled by salt. Saul reached for it, curiosity outweighing his exhaustion. The bottle was heavy, heavier than it should be for its size. There was something inside, something that rattled when he shook it. He frowned, feeling a strange heat pulse against his palm. A whisper, almost imperceptible, curled around the edges of his mind, a voice like wind rustling through dried leaves.

"Set me free..."

Saul blinked, heart pounding. It must have been the wind playing tricks on him. He stuffed the bottle into his satchel and rowed back to shore.

That evening, after laying his daughter to bed, Saul sat at the worn kitchen table, the bottle before him. Celeste watched warily as he toyed with the cork. "You should leave it be," she murmured. "Old folks say some bottles float for a reason."

"It's just an old bottle," Saul scoffed. "Might be worth something."

With a grunt, he pulled the cork free.

A hiss escaped the bottle, like steam from a boiling pot. The lantern light flickered as a shadow slithered out, stretching unnaturally before coalescing into a small, wiry creature no taller than a child. Its skin was the colour of damp bark, with eyes too large, too bright, and gleaming with mischief.

Celeste gasped, clutching her belly. "Bacoo," she whispered in terror.

The Bacoo grinned, revealing sharp, needle-like teeth. "You have freed me, fisherman," it crooned, its voice both playful and menacing. "And for that, I grant you fortune beyond measure."

Saul hesitated. "Fortune?"

The Bacoo nodded eagerly. "Gold. Fish to fill your nets. No hunger, no want. But you must feed me, house me, keep me close. A small price, yes?"

Greed and desperation warred in Saul's chest. He thought of Celeste, his unborn child, his debts. Slowly, he nodded.

The Bacoo clapped its gnarled hands, laughing. "Wise choice, fisherman."

And so, it began.

At first, fortune did indeed smile upon them. Saul's nets overflowed with fish, and the market paid handsomely. He found gold coins nestled in the sand beneath his feet, his pockets never empty. Their home filled with luxuries once unimaginable.

But the Bacoo was never satisfied. It gorged on milk and bananas, but its hunger grew. It whispered in Saul's ear at night, filling his dreams with shadows and hints of deeper, darker desires. Its laughter echoed in the walls, its eyes ever-watchful.

Then came the mischief. Tools misplaced. Food spoiled overnight. The neighbours' animals were found dead with their throats slit, their blood staining the doorstep. Celeste begged Saul to cast the creature away, but he could not bring himself to let go of his newfound prosperity.

Until the night he found his daughter's bed empty.

A trail of small, wet footprints led outside, toward the sea.

Saul ran, breath ragged, heart hammering. The Bacoo sat atop a rock by the shore, cradling his daughter in its spindly arms. She slept, unnaturally still.

"Why do you fight, fisherman?" it whispered. "She is a gift, as you were to me. A bond is made. You are mine, as she shall be."

Rage overtook Saul. He lunged, grasping the Bacoo by its throat. The creature shrieked, writhing in his grip, its form shifting like smoke. He grabbed the bottle from his satchel and, with every ounce of strength, forced the wriggling demon back inside.

The wind howled as he sealed the cork.

Breathing hard, he looked at his daughter. She stirred, opening her eyes. "Papa?"

Tears blurred his vision. "I'm here, baby."

With the first light of dawn, Saul rowed far into the sea and hurled the cursed bottle into the deep, watching it sink beneath the waves, taking with it the whispers and the greed that had almost cost him everything.

But as the sun rose, he swore he heard the faintest of laughs carried upon the wind.

"The Bacoo always waits."

How Spaniards Were Found To Be Mortal

This story has been adapted from an original tale in Charles M. Skinner's book, Myths & Legends of our New Possessions & Protectorate, published by J. B. Lippincott Company, Philadelphia & London, 1900.

Long ago, when the great ships with their billowing white sails first arrived on the shores of the Caribbean, the people of the islands looked upon the strangers with awe and reverence. They believed these pale men had descended from the heavens, their glistening armour and powerful weapons marking them as gods. How else could one explain the thunder that roared from their hands or the fire that danced upon their swords?

At first, the islanders welcomed them with open hearts. They offered their finest fruits, the softest hammocks, the rarest gold from the rivers, believing the gifts would be met with kindness. But the men from across the sea, led by their own greedy kings, desired more. More gold. More land. More power.

Among these conquerors was a man called Don Sebastián Salzedo, a captain with cold eyes and a hunger that could not be satisfied. He, like the others, encouraged the people's belief in their divinity, allowing them to bow and serve, offering them baubles and beads in return for treasures beyond measure. But as the seasons passed, the islanders began to see the truth behind their golden lie. These gods bled.

Their weapons spit thunder, but their flesh was weak. They struck with fire, but they feared the storms that lashed the shores. They built fortresses, but they trembled at the night cries of the jungle. Perhaps they were not gods after all.

Among those who came to doubt was Agueynaba, a great cacique, a leader whose people had suffered beneath the strangers' rule. He watched as his brothers were forced to dig the earth, their hands worn raw as they pulled gold from the rivers for their cruel masters. He saw the once-proud warriors broken, their strength drained in service to men who took everything and gave nothing.

Agueynaba called his council together beneath the towering ceiba tree. "If they are gods," he said, "then they cannot die. And if they are men, then they can be unmade. Let us see which they truly are."

One evening, under the guise of obedience, Agueynaba and his warriors prepared a great journey for Don Salzedo. The captain, eager to expand his dominion, set out with a small band of his men, trusting the islanders to guide him safely through the rivers and hills. He did not see the glances exchanged between his escorts, nor did he question their smiles, which hid the fire of vengeance behind their teeth.

When they came to a river, wide and deep, the warriors offered to carry him across upon their shoulders, just as they had done for many others. Proud and unwary, Don Salzedo allowed himself to be lifted, his armour gleaming in the sun. Halfway across, the warriors let him slip.

The water closed over him in an instant. He thrashed, gasping as the river swallowed his cries, his heavy armour dragging him down. The warriors held him beneath the surface, their hands like the weight of all the lives he had taken. Minutes passed. Then an hour. Then two. When at last they pulled him from the water, he lay limp and lifeless, his once-mighty form nothing more than a drowned man.

The warriors stood in silence, their breath held in their chests. They had expected fire from the sky, or the earth to split open in rage, but nothing happened. The birds still sang, the trees still swayed in the breeze, the river still ran to the sea. The man they had called a god had died like any other.

News of Salzedo's death spread across the islands like the wind before a storm. No longer did the people cower beneath the lash of their oppressors. No longer did they tremble at the sound of foreign tongues. If one Spaniard could die, then so could the others. And so they fought back.

The mountains became their sanctuaries, the rivers their allies, the forests their weapons. The Spaniards, though strong, were few. And now, they were afraid. Though they struck down many warriors, more rose in their place, undaunted, for they had seen the truth, the invaders were not gods. They were mortal. And they could fall.

The Exorcist's Daughter

This story has been adapted from an original tale in Herman van Cappelle Jr's book, Myths and legends from the West Indies, published by Zutphen—Wj Thieme & Cie, in 1926. These tales were originally published in the Dutch language.

In a village nestled between the emerald-green hills and the endless blue of the Caribbean sea, there lived a piaiman, a powerful shaman, feared and respected by all. His wisdom could cure the sick, his chants could call the rain, and his spells could ward off evil. But for all his power, there was one thing he could not control, and that was his daughter's heart.

The piaiman's daughter, Anielka, was as radiant as the morning sun, with skin as smooth as cocoa and hair as dark as the night sea. Many young men in the village sought her favour, but she had eyes only for one, a hunter named Ajani.

Ajani was strong and swift, his arrows never missing their mark. He had three faithful hunting dogs, and his name was sung in the village for the feasts his game provided. Yet for all his bravery, he was blind to Anielka's love.

She watched him from afar, her heart as heavy as stone. When he returned from the hunt, she longed to welcome him home, to prepare his meals, and to share in his triumphs. But he never noticed her, nor did he ever say more than a passing word to her.

Desperate, Anielka went to her father. "Father," she pleaded, "I love Ajani, but he does not see me. He should have a wife who waits for him, and who tends to his home when he returns weary from the hunt. Let me be that woman."

The piaiman looked into her tear-streaked face and sighed deeply. "Daughter, love should not be won by tricks and spells."

"But Father, if I cannot be his wife," she wept, "then let me be by his side in any way I can. Let me go with him into the jungle, let me run beside him as his loyal companion."

The piaiman considered her words, then reached into a chest of ancient relics. From it, he withdrew a dog skin, smooth and brown, and handed it to her. "Take this," he said, "and wear it over your shoulders. If this is your heart's true desire, then let it be so. But be warned, love won through magic is a love as unsteady as a canoe in a storm."

Anielka clutched the skin to her chest, whispered her thanks, and draped it over herself. In an instant, her body changed. Her hands curled into paws, her voice turned to a bark, and her keen eyes took on the golden glow of a hunting hound. She ran into the forest, swift and eager, and joined Ajani's pack. From that day on, Ajani hunted with four dogs at his side, but he never knew that one of them was not truly a beast.

Every afternoon, as the sun began to lower, one of the dogs would slip away. It would not fight with the others, nor would it chase the deer or wild boar. Instead, it would vanish into the trees, running back to the hut.

And there, a miracle would occur. When Ajani returned from the jungle, he always found his home warm and welcoming. The fire would be burning, his cassava bread freshly baked, his hammock neatly arranged. Everything was perfect.

At first, he thought a kind neighbour had taken pity on his lonely existence. But when he asked, no one knew anything of it. "It must be the work of some wandering spirit," he murmured to himself one evening.

As he said these words, one of his dogs looked at him strangely, as though it wanted to speak but could not. A feeling of unease settled over him. The next morning, as he prepared for the hunt, he counted his dogs. There were only three.

"Where has my fourth hound gone?" he muttered.

Determined to find out, he set a trap. Pretending to leave for the hunt, he crept silently through the trees and returned to his hut before sunset. And there, before his very eyes, stood the most beautiful woman he had ever seen. She moved with grace, her hands kneading cassava dough with practiced ease. Her dark curls fell over her shoulders, and her golden-brown skin glowed in the firelight. But what caught his breath was what hung beside the door; a dog skin, draped over a wooden post. The truth struck him like a thunderclap. He had been living with a spirit in disguise.

Ajani did not hesitate. He lunged for the dog skin, snatching it from its resting place. The woman turned in shock, her wide eyes filling with fear. "No!" she gasped. "Give it back!"

But Ajani threw it into the fire. The flames devoured it greedily, turning it to ashes in moments. Anielka fell to her knees, weeping as if her heart had shattered.

"Why did you do that?" she sobbed. "Now I cannot hide! Now I must return to my father!"

Ajani's heart ached at her sorrow, but a new understanding had dawned upon him. "No longer will you hide behind magic," he said gently. "No longer will you live as a shadow in my life. I see you now, not as a spirit, not as a dog, but as the woman you are. And I will follow you to your father's house and ask for your hand, for you are the bride I did not know I needed."

Hearing these words, Anielka wiped away her tears. A small, hopeful smile touched her lips. And so, hand in hand, they walked back to the piaiman's hut, where the old shaman was waiting, a knowing look in his wise eyes. He had seen it all before, the way love twists and turns, the way fate bends but never breaks. With a solemn nod, the piaiman gave his blessing.

And so, under the warm Caribbean moon, Ajani and Anielka were wed, not by magic, not by trickery, but by the simple and steadfast love of two souls who had finally found their way to each other. And never again did a dog slip away from Ajani's hunts, for his true companion was waiting at home, in the warmth of their hearth, where love had always meant to be.

Anansi And The Tar-Baby

This story has been adapted from an original tale in Martha Warren Beckwith's book, Jamaica Anansi Stories, published by The American Folk-Lore Society, New York, in 1924. This story is as told by Vivian Bailey, Mandeville.

Long ago, in a little village nestled in the hills of the Santa Cruz Mountains, there lived a clever but mischievous creature named Anansi. Now, Anansi was not quite man, nor quite beast, he was something in between: a spider of many legs, many schemes, and even more tricks.

One dry season, Tiger, the proud and powerful overseer of the village lands, planted a field full of sweet peas. Wanting someone to watch over his crop, he asked Anansi to be his watchman. "You'll guard my peas, won't you?" Tiger growled. "Make sure no thief puts their hand on them."

"Oh, certainly, Brother Tiger," said Anansi, bowing low with a grin too wide to be honest. "I'll guard it with my very life."

But Anansi was greedy. And every night, while pretending to watch over the field, he helped himself to handfuls of sweet peas, stuffing his belly full until he could barely wobble home.

Tiger grew suspicious. So one night, he took a thick tree stump and smeared it all over with sticky tar. Then, to fool the thief, he placed a broad straw hat upon it and left it right in the middle of the field.

The next night, along came Anansi again, humming a tune and licking his lips in anticipation of another bellyful of peas. But when he reached the field, he stopped. There stood a figure, wearing a wide-brimmed hat, standing still in the middle of the pea patch.

"Who's that in the field?" Anansi called.

No reply.

Anansi stepped closer. "I said, who are you?"

Still no reply.

He poked the figure with his right hand, and it stuck.

"Let me go!" he cried. "You want to hold me? Fine, I'll use my left hand too!"

He slapped the stump with his left hand, and it stuck too.

"You think that's funny, eh? You hold my hands, I'll buck you with my head!"

He headbutted the stump, and his forehead stuck firm.

"Well then! I'll kick you next!" he shouted, now quite furious.

He kicked the stump with his right foot, it stuck. Then the left, stuck fast as well.

Now, completely glued to the tar-covered stump, Anansi sighed and muttered, "Poor me. Now look at that, I'm a watchman, and you're a watchman. Hmmm… well, we're both working now."

And then he began to sing:

"Me deh 'pon duty, but me can't move.

Tar keep me tight, Lord, what a groove!"

By morning, Tiger returned to the field and saw Anansi stuck fast to the stump. "Well, well, Brother Anansi," said Tiger, grinning. "So it was you mashin' up my peas all this time?"

He peeled Anansi from the stump and held him high. "Now what should I do with you, hmm?"

Anansi, being as clever as ever, widened his eyes and pleaded, "Please, Brother Tiger, don't burn me. Whatever you do, don't throw me in the fire!"

Tiger's eyes lit up. "Burn you? Yes, that sound like a fine idea."

So he built a big fire, and just as he was about to toss Anansi into the flames, Anansi said, "No, no, Brother Tiger! You don't know how to burn someone properly. You have to jump over the fire three times first. That's the right way!"

Tiger blinked. "Is that so?"

"Yes, yes," Anansi said eagerly. "Jump three times. Then it'll work."

So Tiger leapt over the fire once, then twice, but as he was preparing for his third grand leap, Anansi, quick as lightning, twisted round, kicked Tiger hard, and knocked him into the flames.

"YOWWW!" Tiger howled, and Anansi darted away into the hills, laughing all the way back to the pea patch, where he finished off every last pod in peace.

The Whispering Mangroves

I've collected versions of this tale from various online and paper sources and this story is my own telling of the legend of the Chickcharney. The Chickcharney is mostly associated with The Bahamas, and Andros island in particular.

The island of Andros Island was untouched, and possessed places where no human dared to tread. Fishermen spoke of strange things among the trees, their voices hushed over glasses of rum in the flickering glow of oil lamps. Travelers swore they had seen something with luminous red eyes watching them from the darkness.

Jabari Sinclair was a researcher from Kingston, and he didn't believe in ghosts and ghouls. He had spent years studying the natural world, debunking myths and chasing legends only to find nothing but superstition. Now, his latest obsession had brought him to Andros Island, a place of untamed wilderness and whispered warnings.

The locals had tried to dissuade him.

"Do not disrespect the Chickcharney," an old woman warned him at the market, her gnarled fingers wrapped around a bundle of herbs. "It is older than the trees, and hungrier than the sea."

Jabari had smiled politely, chalking it up to island superstition.

Now, deep in the pine forests, he was alone. The air was thick with the scent of salt and wet earth, the buzzing of unseen insects filling the heavy night air. His boots sank into the mud as he adjusted his backpack, scanning the twisted roots for any sign of movement.

That's when he saw it.

A hollow in the trunk of a massive silk cotton tree, dark and gaping like an open mouth. Bones, small and brittle, were scattered at its base, tangled with beads and tattered cloth. Jabari's pulse quickened. He raised his camera, adjusting the focus. If this was a sign of the Chickcharney's lair, then he would be the first to document it.

A rustling sound came from above him. Jabari slowly turned his head to see what was making this noise. Perched on a low-hanging branch was a figure unlike anything he had ever seen. It was small, frail even, its skin wrinkled and stretched tight over its bones. At first glance Jabari thought he was looking at a strange sort of owl, but then he started to lose himself in the creature's mesmerising eyes…

Two enormous, glowing red orbs locked onto his own, unblinking, filled with something ancient and insatiable. A wave of nausea washed over him. His limbs felt sluggish, his thoughts heavy.

The Chickcharney tilted its head, a grotesque, birdlike motion. Its cracked lips twisted into something almost like a grin. Then, it moved. Faster than he thought possible, it dropped from the tree, scuttling across the forest ground on all fours. Jabari stumbled back, breath catching in his throat.

Snap.

A sharp pain tore through his leg.

Looking down, he saw a root curled around his ankle, tightening. No, not a root. A long, sinewy finger.

More rustling. More glowing eyes peering from the pines.

Jabari's breath came in panicked gasps. He had made a terrible mistake. The old woman's words rang in his mind. Do not disrespect the Chickcharney.

He had trespassed. He had come uninvited.

And now, he would never leave.

The last thing he saw was the glint of jagged, yellowed teeth stretching into an unnatural grin, strands of viscous saliva snapping between them as the creature's mouth widened beyond the limits of flesh. Its skin cracked and split with a sickening tear, peeling away in curling strips that dripped with thick, dark ichor. Beneath, something pulsed and writhed, its sinewy form glowing with an infernal heat, embers seething beneath raw, exposed muscle. The stench of burning flesh filled his nostrils, his final breath choked by the scent of his own impending death. The creature let out a guttural hiss, its clawed fingers twitching in anticipation, before lunging forward. Blood and darkness.

Then, the forest fell silent once more.

The Water Caves Of Puerto Rico

This story has been adapted from an original tale in Charles M. Skinner's book, Myths & Legends of our New Possessions & Protectorate, published by J. B. Lippincott Company, Philadelphia & London, 1900.

Long ago, in the days when the Spanish flag cast its shadow over the golden shores of Boriquén, there lived a maiden of the Taíno people. She was known as Marielis, a young woman with hair like the flowing rivers and eyes as deep as the ocean. She was the pride of her father, a respected cacique, who had sworn his loyalty only to his people and their gods. But Marielis carried a secret, one that would doom her to an eternity of sorrow.

Among the conquistadors of Ponce de León, there was a young soldier named Diego Velásquez, who had grown weary of war. Unlike his brethren, who sought only gold and conquest, Diego had come to love the land, the sky, the forests, and most of all, Marielis. Their meetings were stolen moments beneath the moonlit canopy of the ceiba trees, away from the hatred that divided their worlds. He swore he would forsake his sword, renounce his allegiance to the Spanish crown, and take her far away, where neither war nor duty could separate them.

But love, in such times, was a dangerous thing. One fateful evening, Marielis' father discovered their secret. His rage was like the tempest, for to love an invader was to betray her people. He forbade her from ever seeing Diego again, vowing that if he laid eyes upon the Spaniard, his spear would find his heart before another sunset.

But love laughs at warnings. Determined to see her beloved once more, Marielis led Diego to a hidden place in the limestone hills, where the earth had hollowed itself into three deep pools. The largest of them, a pool as dark as midnight, concealed a secret, a cave beneath the waters. She had used it before, slipping into the waters to disappear when her father's men came searching. It was their sanctuary, a place known only to them.

That night, as they sat upon the rocky edge, whispering promises of escape, the winds carried footsteps. Her father had followed her. A warning cry was all she could manage before Diego was seized, his arms wrenched behind him. The old cacique's eyes burned with fury, his warriors' spears gleaming in the dim light.

"This is how you honour your ancestors?" he spat, his voice shaking. "By lying with those who bring death to our people?"

Marielis threw herself before Diego, her hands clasped together in a desperate plea. "Father, please! I love him!"

But the words only hardened his heart. A command was given. Two warriors seized Diego by the arms and dragged him toward the deepest of the pools. The Spaniard struggled, his cries for Marielis echoing through the hills. The soldiers forced him to his knees at the edge, and before he could fight back, they shoved him into the abyss.

The water swallowed him whole. Marielis screamed, breaking free from her father's grasp. She ran to the edge, but all that remained was a ripple distorting the reflection of the moon. There was no thrashing, no sign of movement, only the silent embrace of the deep. Her heart shattered. The air felt too heavy to breathe, the stars above seeming to flicker and dim as if they, too, mourned. A great wail erupted from her lips, a song of grief that the wind carried to the mountains.

Then, without hesitation, she leapt into the water. She dove deep, searching, her fingers reaching for him in the endless dark. But Diego had already sunk, the weight of his armour pulling him into the unknown. She found him at last, his lifeless face frozen in sorrow, his hand outstretched toward her as if he had been reaching for her even in his final moments.

She would not leave him again. Wrapping her arms around him, she let herself sink, allowing the water to claim her as well. Her eyes never left his, even as the last breath left her lips. And so, in death, as in life, they remained together.

Yet their story did not end there. To this day, the people of Ponce whisper of two figures that emerge from the waters on moonless nights. Shadowy shapes, tinged in a soft blue glow, seated at the edge of the cavern pool with arms entwined. They say that those who wander too close to the cave can still hear Marielis' sorrowful song, drifting over the hills like mist. Some even claim that the waters remain unnaturally cold, no matter the season, as if still touched by the presence of those long lost beneath its surface.

Many travellers come to the Water Caves, some seeking treasure, others drawn by the lure of legend. Few leave unchanged. For in the stillness of the pools, when the night is at its quietest, one can almost hear a whisper on the wind, a voice calling from the depths:

"Mi amor... do not leave me again..."

The Spirit Of A Fungus Plant Saves A Girl

This story has been adapted from an original tale in Herman van Cappelle Jr's book, Myths and legends from the West Indies, published by Zutphen—Wj Thieme & Cie, in 1926. These tales were originally published in the Dutch language.

Long ago, in a village nestled between emerald hills and swaying palms, there lived two sisters, Amara and Yara. Their mother and father were loving but often absent, leaving the girls to fend for themselves. One evening, the village prepared for a great festival, a night of drumming, dancing, and drinking beneath the stars.

"Come, my daughters," their mother urged. "Join the feast, for the spirits of the ancestors will dance with us tonight!"

But Amara and Yara shook their heads.

"We would rather stay," said Amara, the elder.

"The night belongs to things more than spirits and men," added Yara, younger and wiser in many ways.

Their parents left reluctantly, disappearing along the jungle trails, their laughter fading into the night. The sisters locked the door and sat by the fire, speaking in hushed voices as the moon climbed into the sky. As they sat, a rustling came from the edge of the trees. A shadow emerged from the dark, tall and sinewy, his skin as pale as driftwood, his eyes glinting like fireflies. His hair hung in tangled locks, and around his shoulders, he carried a bow and quiver of arrows.

"Good evening," he said, his voice as smooth as river stones. "I have brought you a gift."

In his hands, he held a freshly killed parrot, its feathers as red as the setting sun.

"I have travelled far from the hills," he continued. "Cook this bird for me, and I shall share my meal with you."

The sisters hesitated. Something in the stranger's gaze sent shivers through their bones, but hunger and curiosity outweighed their caution. They plucked and roasted the parrot, sharing the meal with their visitor. When the last bite was gone, the man stretched lazily and slung a hammock from the rafters of their hut.

"I am weary," he said. "Let one of you keep me company tonight."

Yara tensed, feeling something unnatural in his words, but Amara, eager to show kindness, stepped forward.

"I will," she said, casting her sister a reassuring glance. She climbed into the hammock, and the man rocked it gently, his eyes glittering like a predator's.

As the night stretched on, Yara heard a strange noise. A slow, thick sound, like liquid dripping onto the earth. Then came a whisper, low and pained. Yara's skin prickled. She crept to the fire, stirring the embers to cast more light.

The hammock was soaked in crimson. Blood dripped like candle wax onto the floor, and there, tangled in the fabric, was Amara's lifeless body.

The man was gone.

Yara staggered back, a scream rising in her throat. She recognized now what had been hiding behind that stranger's smile. He was no ordinary man, he was a Joroka, a dark spirit of the forest. Some said the Joroka were demons that fed on the flesh of the innocent. Others claimed they were cursed men, neither living nor dead, forever doomed to wander the night in search of prey.

Yara knew she was next.

She ran from the hut, her breath ragged. She did not flee toward the village, no, the Joroka would expect that. Instead, she ran to the abandoned maize fields where the Fungus Spirit lived. These fields had been abandoned long ago, for the crops had rotted with disease. Now, strange mushrooms sprouted in the moonlight, their white caps glowing like ghostly lanterns. The villagers whispered that a spirit dwelled here, a keeper of rot and renewal, neither kind nor cruel, but powerful.

Panting, Yara fell to her knees among the decaying stalks. "Great Spirit," she whispered, pressing her hands to the damp earth. "I seek your protection. If the Joroka comes for me, do not let him take me. If you save me, I will never steal from your fields. I will leave you offerings of maize and honey. Please, help me!"

The air around her grew thick with the scent of damp earth and moss. A wind stirred through the dying crops. Then, silence. Yara pressed herself into the stalks, barely daring to breathe.

Moments later, the Joroka arrived. His pale face shone in the dark, his eyes gleaming as he sniffed the air like a beast.

"Fungus Spirit," he called, his voice echoing through the field. "Have you seen the girl?"

The wind whispered through the maize, but the Spirit did not answer. The Joroka scoured the field, clawing through the rotting stalks, but he found nothing. At dawn, furious and empty-handed, he vanished back into the jungle.

When the sun was high, Yara crept out of her hiding place. Shaken but alive, she followed the winding path back to her village. There, she found her parents and the villagers, just returning from their night of revelry. When she saw them, grief overcame her, and she wailed, "The Joroka took my sister!"

Her mother clutched her chest. "You should have come with us!" she lamented.

Yara led them to the hut, but when they searched, there was no trace of Amara's body. Only the stained hammock remained, swaying in the morning breeze. The villagers seethed with rage. They would not let the demon escape.

"We must find the Komaka tree," Yara said, remembering the signs of the Joroka's tribe. "That is where he lives."

At once, the villagers gathered baskets of red pepper pods, the strongest weapon they had against spirits. They travelled deep into the jungle until they found the ancient Komaka tree, its thick branches twisting toward the sky like grasping fingers.

A fire was built around its base, and the villagers scattered the peppers into the flames. The air filled with thick, choking smoke.

From the treetops came a terrible wailing. Then, a swarm of small creatures, twisted things, half-human and half-beast, scrambled down the branches, coughing and screeching. The villagers did not hesitate. They struck them down with spears and clubs, their fury unmatched. More peppers were thrown into the fire. More creatures fell. Then, at last, the Joroka himself emerged.

He was monstrous in the daylight, his skin now as grey as death, his mouth twisted into a snarl. But he was no match for the rage of a grieving father.

"You stole my daughter!" Amara's father bellowed, raising his spear.

The villagers descended upon the Joroka. He howled as their blades cut him down, and when his body was split open, the flesh of his past victims spilled onto the earth.

At last, the demon was dead.

From that day forward, Yara obeyed her parents without question. She never again stayed alone at night. She never entered the forest unaccompanied. And every season, she left offerings of maize and honey in the rotting fields, where the Fungus Spirit had once saved her life.

Even now, under the Caribbean moon, some say the Joroka still lurks in the deepest jungles, waiting for foolish souls who wander alone. And those who dare to walk the shadowed paths should remember, the spirits of the land are always watching.

Doba

This story has been adapted from an original tale in Walter Jekyll's book, Jamaican Song And Story, published by David Nutt, London,, in 1907.

One day, Cat decided to throw a grand ball and invited every rat in the land. All the rats came dressed to the nines, long coats, silk dresses, thousands of them, both men and women. They even brought their children: a little boy rat, his mother, and her newborn baby.

Once everyone was inside, the doors were shut. But what no one knew was that the cats had hidden clubs up their trouser legs. They had secretly agreed amongst themselves that once the rats were fully caught up in the dancing, their friend Doba would put out the lights, then the ambush would begin.

When the music started, it was so lively and sweet that the rats danced until their shirts were soaked with sweat.

The fiddler was Dandy Jimmy Flint. And this is what his fiddle played:

"Doba, Doba, Doba, don't let the little ones escape!

Ballantony Bap! twee twee,

Ballantony Bap! twee twee!"

Now, the young boy rat was clever, and he paid close attention to what the fiddle was saying. He tugged on his father's coat and whispered, "Papa, did you hear what the fiddle just said?"

"Doba, Doba, Doba, don't let the little ones escape!

Ballantony Bap! twee twee,

Ballantony Bap! twee twee!"

But the father snapped at him, "Oh, be quiet, you silly little thing! This is exactly why you shouldn't bring children to big events. Go away with your nonsense!"

But the boy rat was no fool. He heard the warning loud and clear. So, while the others danced, he quietly dug a hole in the corner of the hall, just big enough for himself, his mother, and the baby.

When the rats were deep into their dancing, gatekeeper Doba, who was also a cat, suddenly put out the lamp. The hall went dark. And then the clubs came flying. Whack! Smash! Crash! The cats laid into the rats, beating and killing them. Blood covered the floor. The cats took their share of meat and feasted.

Only the boy rat, his mother, and the baby escaped, through the hole he had dug. If the father had listened to his son, he wouldn't have died.

The Cat's ball ended in a blood-soaked banquet. And if the boy rat and his mother hadn't escaped, there'd be no rats left in this world at all.

The Riddle

This story has been adapted from an original tale in Martha Warren Beckwith's book, Jamaica Anansi Stories, published by The American Folk-Lore Society, New York, in 1924. This story is as told by Vivian Bailey, Mandeville.

In the days when the world was still filled with magic and men could talk with animals, Anansi the spider wasn't just a trickster, he was a master of stories, a weaver of cleverness, and a friend who always found a way, even in the darkest of times.

One day, news came to Anansi that his good friend Tacoomah had been arrested. The authorities had tried him for a crime, and the king had ordered that he be hanged at dawn.

Now, Anansi wasn't the sort to sit back and let a friend suffer, not if he could help it. That evening, he slipped into the court of the king, all smiles and charm. The palace guards knew better than to trust Anansi, but no one could deny his way with words. He bowed low and said to the king, "Your Majesty, I beg a word."

The king raised a brow. "It better be a good one, Anansi. Your friend's fate is sealed."

Anansi grinned. "What if I gave Your Majesty a riddle? One so clever, so cunning, that if you cannot solve it, you'll let Tacoomah go free?"

The king, proud and fond of riddles, leaned forward. "Very well. If your riddle bests me, he walks free. But if I solve it, he hangs by morning."

Anansi bowed again, but this time more deeply. "Then it's a deal, Your Majesty." Then he scurried away as fast as his eight little legs could carry him.

Back at Tacoomah's hut, Anansi found his friend pacing. "Brother Anansi," Tacoomah said, wringing his hands, "what did the king say?"

"Don't worry yourself, Brother Tacoomah," said Anansi with a wink. "I've struck a deal. If we give him a riddle he can't solve, you go free."

Tacoomah's face lit with hope, then darkened again. "But what riddle could be clever enough to trick a king?"

Anansi's eyes gleamed. "Leave that to me, but you must do exactly as I say."

Tacoomah nodded quickly. "Anything, Brother Anansi. Just save my life."

Anansi led Tacoomah to the back of his small holding, where a mare heavy with foal stood grazing. "We'll need her," Anansi said quietly.

And what followed was strange magic. They gently laid the mare down, and Anansi, with great care, opened her belly and delivered the colt, who blinked at the world as though waking from a dream. From a strip of the mare's skin, Anansi fashioned a fine bridle. The mare was buried with honour, for in death she had become part of a tale that would outlive them all.

Next, Anansi instructed Tacoomah to fill his hat with fresh earth from beneath a silk cotton tree, the kind the spirits liked best. Then he placed a silver coin in one boot and a gold coin in the other. Tacoomah mounted the colt, who had never seen the light of day until that very night, and Anansi handed him the mare-skin bridle.

"Now ride to the palace, Brother Tacoomah," said Anansi, "and when the king asks for your riddle, you say these words exactly as I taught you."

Tacoomah rode at dawn, and when he arrived at the palace, he was met with curious eyes. No one had seen a man ride a colt so young nor wear such a strange look of calm before a king.

He stood tall before the throne, tipped his dirt-filled hat, and recited:

"Under the earth I stood,

Silver and gold were my tread,

I rode a thing that never was born,

And a bit of the dam I hold in my hand."

The king leaned back, his fingers steepled. "Hmm," he said. "A clever rhyme. But what does it mean?"

For hours the court whispered and puzzled, until the king finally admitted defeat. "Explain it," he commanded, "and it had better be the truth."

Tacoomah obeyed. He took off his hat and let the fresh earth spill out. "Under the earth I stood," he said, "for I filled my hat with the soil of the land."

He raised one boot, then the other. "Silver and gold were my tread. I stood on wealth, silver in one boot, gold in the other."

He patted the colt's neck. "I rode a thing that was never born, for this foal was taken from its mother's belly before it could ever breathe its first breath."

Finally, he held up the bridle. "And this, Your Majesty, is a bit of the dam, his mother, whose skin I hold in my hand."

There was silence in the court.

Then the king laughed. Not just a polite chuckle, but a deep, rolling laugh that shook the rafters. "You crafty devil," he said. "Only Anansi could cook up a riddle like that. Go on, both of you, get out of my court before I change my mind."

And just like that, Tacoomah was free.

As they left the palace, Anansi clapped a hand on his friend's shoulder and grinned. "See, Brother Tacoomah? Never doubt a spider with a sharp tongue and a clever mind."

And from that day to this, folks still say: when all seems lost, find yourself an Anansi, because he'll spin a story that just might save your life.

The Curse Of The Silk Cotton Tree

I've collected versions of this tale from various online and paper sources and this story is my own telling of the legend of Silk Cotton Tree. The Silk Cotton Tree is deeply rooted in Caribbean folklore, with legends associated with several islands, particularly: Jamaica, Trinidad and Tobago, Haiti, The Bahamas, and The Virgin Islands. The Silk Cotton Tree is frequently seen as a home for spirits, particularly the restless souls of the dead, and is often tied to African and Indigenous spiritual beliefs, acting as a sacred bridge between realms. The tree is feared and respected, and those who attempt to cut it down or disturb it often suffer bad luck, misfortune, or supernatural encounters.

The Silk Cotton Tree loomed over the village like an ancient guardian, its gnarled roots twisting through the earth like the fingers of a buried giant. It stood at the edge of the forest, a place of silent reverence and quiet fears. The villagers of Bellamy Parish knew better than to step too close, especially after nightfall.

They said that the tree was older than time itself, its roots a dwelling place for restless spirits, the ghosts of those who had died in torment, their wails trapped within the bark, their sorrow seeping into the air like mist at dusk. Generations had passed down the warnings: Do not touch the roots. Do not break a branch. Do not anger the spirits.

But when Richard Laveau, a sceptical outsider, arrived in the village, he dismissed their fears as backward superstition. He was a developer with grand plans. He wanted to clear the land and build a resort, a place of luxury and modernity, where tourists could sip cocktails under the same sky where the ancestors once danced.

Old Mother Benet, the village elder, spat at his feet the first time he spoke of cutting down the tree. "You do not know what you speak of," she rasped. Her face, a map of wrinkles and wisdom, darkened with fury. "That tree holds more than roots, boy. It holds the dead. And the dead do not like to be disturbed."

Richard laughed her off. "It's just a tree," he scoffed. "And it's coming down."

That night, the wind howled through the village like a warning. The sky, once clear, darkened with an unnatural storm. Richard, ever the defiant fool, took an axe and a lantern and marched up to the Silk Cotton Tree. His first strike against the bark sent an eerie vibration through the ground, as though the earth itself had gasped in pain. The lantern flickered, and in its dim glow, shadows slithered along the tree's massive trunk.

He swung again.

A sound like a woman's wail cut through the night. He froze, his breath catching in his throat. From the roots, mist curled upward, thick and suffocating. Faces began to form in the haze, twisted, anguished, their eyes hollowed pits of endless suffering.

Then, he heard a distinct a whisper: "You should not have come."

Richard's shivered as terror seized his body. He turned, his heart hammering in his chest, his legs burning with the urgency to flee. But just as he took his first desperate step, something latched onto his ankle. He looked down and saw a moving root. It coiled around him like a living thing, rough bark grinding against his skin. The grip tightened instantly, cutting off his circulation, and before he could even process what was happening, it pulled.

Richard's scream tore through the night, but there was no one to hear it. He thrashed violently, digging his fingers into the dirt, clawing at the tangled roots around him. His nails split, blood seeping into the soil. He kicked at the gnarled limb holding him, but with every struggle, it only constricted further, twisting like a snake sinking its fangs deeper into its prey.

More roots erupted from the earth, writhing like long, pale fingers reaching for him. They slithered over his arms, his chest, his throat. Panic surged as they pulled again, dragging him toward the monstrous trunk.

"No...no, please!" he choked out, his voice hoarse, his cries swallowed by the oppressive silence of the forest.

Then he saw them. The tree was no longer just a tree. It watched him. From within the bark, faces emerged, dozens, no, hundreds, twisting in agony. Hollowed-out eyes stared at him, their expressions frozen in an eternal scream, their mouths gaping black voids, their features contorted in pain. Some were barely formed, their flesh melding into the wood as though they had been absorbed, and trapped in an endless torment.

He tried to look away, but the faces moved. Mouths stretched wider, grinning in unnatural ways. Lips peeled back over jagged, splintered teeth. Eyes that should have been empty flickered with something not quite human, something hungry, something ancient.

The roots yanked him harder. His body lurched forward, his face scraping against the dirt. He felt something wet beneath him. The soil was dark and thick, not just mud, but something else. Something coppery, something warm. Blood.

The tree fed.

Richard sobbed, his mind screaming for escape. He reached for anything to stop himself from being pulled under. His hands slapped against a jagged piece of stone, and with one final, desperate attempt, he slammed it against the root coiling around his leg.

A shriek tore through the air. The tree screamed. The sound was unlike anything human, a shrill, keening wail that vibrated through his skull. The bark shuddered, the faces writhing, their mouths gasping in silent agony. But the roots did not loosen. If anything, they pulled harder.

Richard's body lurched downward, his torso now engulfed by the earth, his head tilted back as he fought against the inevitable. The last thing he saw was the faces, now so close that he could feel their breath, hot, fetid, and rancid.

The mouths opened wider. They spoke, but not in words. The sound was wet, guttural, like bone scraping against bone, like voices that had long forgotten how to form speech.

And then the darkness took him. The soil surged over his face, stuffing his mouth, filling his nose, crushing his ribs. The tree had claimed him. And the whispering screams of those who had come before him were the only thing that remained.

By morning, the Silk Cotton Tree stood as it always had, ancient, watchful, undisturbed. The only sign of Richard's fate was his lantern, still burning weakly at the base, and the faint hint of laughter rustling through the leaves.

When the villagers found the lantern, Old Mother Benet only nodded, her voice a whisper of prophecy fulfilled. "The tree takes what it is owed."

And from that day forward, no one spoke of removing the tree again, for they knew that some things are not meant to be disturbed.

And the spirits of the Silk Cotton Tree never, ever forget or forgave.

Mateo And The Mermaids

This story has been adapted from an original tale in Charles M. Skinner's book, Myths & Legends of our New Possessions & Protectorate, published by J. B. Lippincott Company, Philadelphia & London, 1900.

In the warm turquoise waters of the Caribbean, where the moonlight drapes silver across the waves and the trade winds whisper secrets through the palms, there are tales as old as the tides themselves. Among them is the legend of the Sea Maidens, creatures of beauty and peril, who lure men into the depths, never to return.

Long before the Spanish fleets came, long before the sugarcane fields stretched across the islands, the people of the coast knew of the Zemi of the Deep, spirits that dwelled beneath the waves. Fishermen claimed to hear their voices on nights when the wind was still, a melody floating over the sea, so beautiful it could steal a man's soul.

"Do not listen," the elders warned. "The mermaids sing not for love, but for hunger."

But some men could not help themselves. And so, there were stories. One such tale tells of Mateo, a fisherman from the shores of Hispaniola, who, against the warnings of his village, went out beyond the reef one night. The sea was like black glass, and the stars reflected upon it as if the heavens had fallen into the water. As he cast his net, the song began, a sound both sorrowful and sweet, like the whisper of the waves themselves.

Then, he saw her. She sat on a rock near the mouth of a cave, her long hair glistening like woven moonlight, her skin kissed by the golden glow of the lantern at his bow. Her eyes, deep and as dark as the ocean before a storm, held him fast. Her lips curled into a smile that promised both wonder and ruin.

"Come closer, fisherman," she called. "The sea is lonely tonight."

Mateo knew the stories, but the sight of her robbed him of reason. He took up his oars and rowed toward her, his heart hammering in his chest, each stroke pulling him closer to the unknown.

As he neared, the maiden rose slightly from the water, revealing her form. She was as the old tales had told, woman to the waist, but below, the body of a great fish, scales shimmering with an unnatural light. Mateo should have turned back. He should have fled. But instead, he reached out his hand.

The mermaid's fingers closed around his wrist, her nails digging into his flesh like tiny hooks. The song stopped. A great silence fell over the sea, and Mateo realized, too late, that the song had not been for him, it had been for his soul.

With a strength no creature should possess, she pulled him forward, her smile widening, revealing teeth, not small, delicate pearls, but sharp, jagged as coral, made for tearing, made for feasting. Mateo screamed as he fought against her grip, but the sea itself seemed to betray him. The water rose up in a sudden surge, the sky above swallowed by rolling mist. His boat tilted, and before he could call for the Virgin's mercy, the ocean claimed him.

The villagers found his boat the next morning, drifting aimlessly near the cove. There was no sign of Mateo. Only his net remained, tangled and torn, as if something monstrous had thrashed against it. And yet, sometimes, when the night is still, the fishermen say they can hear his voice, calling out from beneath the waves, begging for release.

Isabella And The Mermaids

This story has been adapted from an original tale in Charles M. Skinner's book, Myths & Legends of our New Possessions & Protectorate, published by J. B. Lippincott Company, Philadelphia & London, 1900.

Not all mermaids lured their prey from the shore. Some, they say, walked among us.

There was once a young woman named Isabela, a beauty from the island of Puerto Rico, who was known to walk the beaches alone, her gaze always fixed on the horizon. Many men sought her hand, but she would have none of them, for her heart belonged to a man of the sea.

One evening, when the tide was low and the sky streaked red with the dying sun, a stranger came to the village. His hair was as dark as wet stone, his skin as smooth as polished driftwood, and his eyes, his eyes held the colour of the deepest waters. He spoke little, but when he looked at Isabela, she felt as if she had known him all her life.

In secret, they met beneath the great ceiba tree by the shore. He told her of a kingdom beneath the waves, where the coral palaces shimmered like jewels, where the sea was never cruel, and the sun never burned. "Come with me," he whispered, "and you will never know sorrow again."

On the night of the full moon, she left her home, her family, and all she had known. She walked into the waves, hand in hand with her lover. The water swallowed her footsteps, and she was never seen again.

But the village elders say that, when the moon is high and the tide is right, a lone figure can be seen standing by the ceiba tree, her wedding veil trailing in the wind, her eyes black as the abyss. She waits, they say, for others to follow. And some do.

The Caribbean waters are beautiful, but they hold secrets darker than the deepest trenches. The old fishermen still whisper to their sons before they first set sail, passing down the warning that their fathers and grandfathers told them:

"Beware the song of the mermaids. Beware the maidens who rise from the deep. For they do not love as we do. They love only the souls they take."

Some laugh at these old tales, dismiss them as folklore and fancy. But then, on certain nights, when the wind dies and the sea is still, a melody drifts across the water, soft, mournful, inviting.

And there is always someone who listens.

Tiger And Anteater

This story has been adapted from an original tale in Herman van Cappelle Jr's book, Myths and legends from the West Indies, published by Zutphen—Wj Thieme & Cie, in 1926. These tales were originally published in the Dutch language.

Long, long ago, when the forests of the Caribbean still resounded with old magic and beasts walked the earth with voices like men, there lived a striped brute of a creature called Tiger. His fur was golden, his eyes sharp as sugarcane blades, and he believed himself the fiercest, strongest, and cleverest beast from island shore to mountain peak.

One morning, as the mist still curled low over the trees and the parrots were just beginning their noisy chatter, Tiger was striding through the deep green woods, tail high, sniffing the air for mischief or meat, whichever he found first. There, waddling through the brush on wide, flat feet, came Tamanoea, the anteater, with a snout as long as a walking stick and claws that curled like coconut fronds.

Tiger narrowed his eyes and grinned a wide, toothy grin. "Well, look what the storm dragged in," he purred. "Tamanoea, you walk like a drunken crab, and your nose looks like it got stretched in your sleep!"

Tamanoea paused, but only flicked an ear. "Say what you like, Tiger," he replied in a slow, calm voice. "My mouth may be narrow, and my toes may point to the moon, but when it comes to eating meat and standing my ground, I can do just as well as you."

Tiger gave a roar of laughter, loud enough to shake a mango loose from the tree. "You? Eat meat? You haven't so much as sniffed a bone! You eat ants and termites and call it a meal!"

"Oh no," said Tamanoea, "just this morning I had the remains of a deer, leftovers, actually. I think it was you who left it behind. Didn't want the chewy parts, hmm?"

Tiger's tail lashed with the insult. "Liar! You wouldn't know the taste of meat if it danced on your tongue!"

"Well," said Tamanoea, scratching the earth with his long claws, "perhaps you need proof. Shall we both provide… evidence?"

Tiger raised a brow. "You mean, ?"

"Yes," said Tamanoea. "We both… relieve ourselves, close our eyes while we do it, and then take a look. Whoever's leavings prove the meatiest wins."

Tiger, eager to show off, agreed at once.

So they sat, side by side under the shade of a gumbo-limbo tree, eyes squeezed shut. But sly Tamanoea, quiet as shadow, peeked through one slit eye, waited till Tiger finished, and with great care and speed, switched their piles.

"Open your eyes!" Tamanoea sang out.

Tiger did, and he stared in disbelief. Tamanoea's offering was thick with bone bits, gristle, and the scent of venison.

Tiger sniffed his own. "But, this doesn't smell right… This is grass! And berries! Never in my life…!"

"You see?" said Tamanoea, beaming. "You're unwell! All fur and no fire! My clumsy feet might splay like a sea crab's, but I walk as fast and fight as fierce as any cat!"

Tiger's ears lay back. His pride had been bruised, and worse, in front of a snouted little beast who ate ants. Rage boiled up in him like a kettle on fire. With a growl, he crouched low and sprang.

But Tamanoea was ready. As Tiger flew through the air, Tamanoea dipped his long head forward and whoosh, dug his claws right into Tiger's ribs. He twisted, rolled, and with a strength none had ever guessed, crushed the beast in a mighty hug. The forest rang with the crack of bones and Tiger lay still.

The birds fell silent. The wind paused. Tamanoea stood slowly, brushing leaves from his fur. He looked down at the lifeless body of Tiger and gave a quiet sigh.

"Big teeth don't make big wisdom," he said, and walked off into the jungle, humming a tune older than stone.

From that day on, the creatures of the Caribbean never again mocked Tamanoea's snout or his slow, swaying walk. And some say, if you listen close on a quiet evening, you can still hear his humming, weaving through the trees like a lullaby for the clever and the underestimated.

Anansi And The Old Lady's Field

This story has been adapted from an original tale in Walter Jekyll's book, Jamaican Song And Story, published by David Nutt, London,, in 1907.

Once upon a time, there was an old lady who tended a beautiful provision field that grew out of the side of a rocky hill. To protect it, she had a watchman, a strange boy with witching powers, known to be no ordinary child.

Now, Anansi the trickster heard about this mysterious boy, and being up to his usual mischief, he decided to invite the boy to his home. When the boy arrived, Anansi greeted him warmly and asked, "What's your name, my friend?"

The boy replied, "My name is John-John Fe-We-Hall." He looked at Anansi suspiciously. "Why do you want to know my name?"

"Oh, don't worry," Anansi said with a grin. "I only asked because I like you so much."

Meanwhile, the old lady had no idea that her watchman had gone to visit Anansi.

Anansi had a son named Tacoma, a clever thief with fingers as fast as lightning. Anansi came up with a sneaky plan. He told Tacoma, "When you see that boy come to the house, slip out the back door, go to the old lady's field, and ruin her crops. Tear them up, one by one."

So, while John-John sat in Anansi's front room, Anansi went to prepare breakfast for him. But the food wasn't just any meal, it had been taken from the old lady's field.

The old lady had cast a special charm on her crops. She declared that if her watchman ever dared to steal from her, the food would make him terribly ill, and she would know at once who the thief was. But the boy, being a witch-child, knew the food Anansi served him was cursed. So when Anansi brought the breakfast and told him to eat, John-John refused.

"Come now," said Anansi sweetly, "don't be afraid. Eat something."

But John-John shook his head. "No."

Annoyed that his plan had failed, Anansi sent a message to the old lady, saying, "Your watchman is cleverer than I thought. He's outsmarted me."

The old lady still didn't know her watchman had gone to Anansi's house. She sent a message back to her field, warning the boy to beware of Anansi and his tricks. But it was too late, the boy was already in Anansi's yard.

Now here's something you should know. The boy was also a flautist. He often played music for the old lady when she wanted to dance.

She had one special tune that she loved to dance to more than any other.

Anansi, sly as ever, begged the boy, "When you go home, will you play that song for me, just once?"

He knew the tune had power. If the old lady heard it, she wouldn't be able to resist dancing. She would spin and twirl and dance with such wild delight that she might not be able to stop.

As the boy walked home, he raised the flute to his lips and began to play the enchanted tune:

Old lady, you love to dance, turn them,

Old lady, you love to dance, turn them,

Turn them, make them lie down, turn them,

Turn them, make them lie down, turn them.

The moment the old lady heard the song drifting through the air, her feet started moving. She spun, she swayed, she twisted and turned. Round and round she danced, faster and faster, until she lost her balance, tumbled from the rocky hill… and fell to her death.

From that day on, Anansi took over the field, and to this very day,

The Cowitch And Mr. Foolman

This story has been adapted from an original tale in Martha Warren Beckwith's book, Jamaica Anansi Stories, published by The American Folk-Lore Society, New York, in 1924. This story is as told by Moses Hendricks, Mandeville.

Once upon a time, in the sun-baked hills just outside Mandeville, there lived a wealthy landowner with a very peculiar problem. On one corner of his estate grew a dense and thorny patch of cowitch, a wicked plant known for its vicious little hairs that made the skin burn and itch like mad if touched. The gentleman had tried everything to get rid of it, but whoever attempted to cut it down ended up scratching themselves to bits. So the gentleman made an offer to the public.

"Anyone who can clear my cowitch patch," he declared, "without scratching themselves once, shall be rewarded with the finest cow from my herd. Your pick of the best."

Naturally, many came to try their luck. Strong men, clever boys, all sorts. But none could endure the sting of the cowitch. They itched and they scratched, and so they failed.

As you might expect, Anansi the trickster caught wind of the challenge. His belly was empty, and the thought of owning a fine cow made his whiskers twitch.

"I'll take the job," he told the landowner, puffing out his chest proudly. "And I'll not scratch once."

The gentleman, suspicious but amused, agreed. He sent his own son to watch Anansi work, just to be sure there was no cheating.

So the next morning, under a blazing sun, Anansi took up his machete and stepped into the cowitch patch. At first, he swung the blade confidently. But before long, the burning itch of the cowitch began to creep up his legs, down his back, along his arms. He gritted his teeth. He wanted so badly to scratch. But he couldn't. But he couldn't, for a boy was watching, his eyes as sharp as hawk talons

Anansi, ever the trickster, decided on a plan. As he swung his blade and the itch worsened, he began to speak. "Young master," he said to the boy, "the cow your father's going to give me, I think she's white along one side," and here he scratched his right side discreetly. "She's black along the other side," and he gave a rub to his left side. "She's also a little red on the rump, another patch of black near the neck, and, ah yes, blue right near her hooves."

He went on like that, describing an imaginary cow while sneakily scratching the itches that tormented him. The boy, too caught up in the colourful picture of the cow, didn't notice a thing.

By sundown, the entire cowitch patch was cleared, and Anansi, itching but victorious, had earned himself the finest cow in the herd.

But now came a new challenge: how to move the cow. Anansi, being small and wiry, couldn't manage it alone. But he didn't want to share his prize with anyone clever. No, he wanted someone foolish, someone he could easily outwit. So he found a man who went by the name Foolman, and asked him for help.

"Brother Foolman," said Anansi, grinning, "help me take this cow down to a spot where we can butcher it and roast the meat."

Foolman agreed. They led the cow away and stopped to make preparations in a clearing not far from Foolman's own yard, though Anansi didn't know that.

"We'll need fire to roast the meat," Anansi said. "You see that smoke in the distance? That's a good place to find it."

Foolman scratched his head and said, "No, no, Brother Nansi. I don't fancy going all that way."

Anansi scowled. "Fine, I'll go myself then," and off he went, grumbling.

But as soon as Anansi disappeared down the path, Foolman's eyes gleamed with mischief.

He whistled sharply, and out came his family. Together, they butchered the cow, stripped it clean, salted the meat, and carted it all off to his yard, just behind the trees. All they left behind was the cow's tail. Then Foolman dug a deep hole and drove the tail into the earth so it stuck up like the cow had vanished underground.

Just before Anansi returned, Foolman grabbed the cow-tail and shouted, "Brother Nansi! Run! Trouble! Brother Nansi, come quick!"

Anansi came dashing through the trees, panting. "What happened?" he cried.

Foolman pointed to the tail. "The cow's gone! She's gone! Down into the ground, only the tail's left!"

Anansi blinked. "Gone? But, but how?"

"We must pull her back up!" Foolman said dramatically, tugging the tail with all his might.

Anansi joined in, and the two of them pulled and pulled… until the tail snapped clean off. Anansi tumbled backwards into the dust, holding nothing but the last hairy bit of his hard-won cow.

And Foolman? Well, he wiped his brow, clutched his belly, and laughed until tears rolled down his cheeks.

That night, Anansi sat alone by his empty fire with only the cow-tail as company. For all his cunning and cleverness, the great trickster had been out-tricked, and by a man named Foolman, no less. And that is how Anansi earned nothing but a tuft of tail for all his scheming, and learned that sometimes, it's the "fool" who has the last laugh.

The Lost Ones Of Black Hollow

I've collected versions of this tale from various online and paper sources and this story is my own telling of the legend of The Douen. The Douen is most associated with Trinidad and Tobago, though similar folklore exists in other parts of the Caribbean.

No one went into Black Hollow after dark. The village elders warned of the things that lived between the trees, their whispers riding the wind like songs half-forgotten. Children who disobeyed and wandered too far never returned, at least, not the way they were before.

Mira's grandmother, as old and as gnarled as the roots of the silk-cotton tree in the village square, had told her stories. The Douen are the lost ones, she would say. They wear wide-brimmed hats to hide their faces, and their feet point backward, so you can never tell where they're truly going. They call out in the voices of the dead, leading the foolish deeper into the trees. The Douen prey on children, and they often take the form of children to appear more appealing.

But stories were stories. And Mira, being sixteen and braver than most, refused to be afraid of things unseen.

That was before her little brother disappeared.

Now it was the third night since Javi had gone missing. He had wandered into the forest after hearing his name being called from the trees. Mira had been the last to see him, standing barefoot at the edge of the hollow, staring into the darkness with wide, glassy eyes. She had called to him, screamed for him to come back, but he didn't even turn around. He had stepped forward, his small body swallowed whole by the forest.

And now, the village had all but given up. "He's gone," the elders said, shaking their heads. "Taken."

But Mira refused to believe that. So, that night, she waited until the village was asleep, took a lantern, and followed the path into Black Hollow. The deeper she went, the quieter it became. The usual chorus of crickets and frogs had disappeared, replaced by the sound of small, shuffling footsteps. Then, she heard a giggle, high and childlike, coming from the trees.

Mira stopped breathing. "Javi?" she whispered.

No answer.

The lantern's glow barely touched the thick trees, but something moved just beyond the light, a shadow, small and round, stepping forward from the underbrush. Mira's pulse pounded as she lifted the lantern higher. It was a child.

A boy, barefoot, wearing tattered clothes. A wide-brimmed straw hat covered most of his face, but his mouth curved into a slow, eerie smile.

Her heart pounded in her chest.

"Javi?" she whispered again.

The boy giggled again and turned, skipping deeper into the woods.

Mira hesitated only a moment before following. The lantern swung wildly in her grasp as she ran after him, calling his name.

"Javi! Stop!"

But he didn't stop. He weaved through the trees effortlessly, as if the forest had no obstacles. It wasn't until she caught a glimpse of his feet that she stumbled to a halt, cold horror washing over her. His feet were backward.

Her brother's face, what little she could see of it, was still smiling, still joyful. But his feet were wrong. Mira took a shaky step back, her instincts screaming at her to run.

"Javi," she said, her voice trembling, "come home with me."

The boy's head tilted slightly, his grin widening.

Then, from all around her, other voices rose. Small, whispering voices. Giggles.

The trees rustled, and from the darkness, more shapes emerged. They were all children. All of them barefoot. All of them grinning beneath their wide hats. And all of them had feet pointing the wrong way.

Mira's breath caught in her throat once more. She took a step back, but the children took a step forward.

"Come play," one of them whispered. "Stay with us."

Their voices blended together in a lilting, hypnotic chorus. "Mira… Mira…" They sang her name, soft and inviting, their laughter bubbling like a stream.

She clutched the lantern, its light flickering. The path she had taken was gone, swallowed by the trees. And then, she felt a tiny, cold hand slipping into hers. She turned her head slowly, her stomach twisting into knots. Javi stood beside her now, his face fully visible.

But it wasn't Javi. His skin was pale, almost grey, and his eyes were hollowed-out pits of black. His smile stretched too wide, too wrong. Mira tried to pull away, but his grip tightened like iron.

"Don't go," he whispered.

The other children crept closer.

The lantern flickered one last time and then died.

In the suffocating dark, Mira heard the children giggling. As much as she wanted to flee the scene, Mira felt utterly compelled to follow the children into the night.

By dawn, the villagers found the lantern, cracked and covered in dirt, lying at the forest's edge.

Mira was never seen again, but on some nights, when the wind carried the laughter of lost children through Black Hollow, the villagers swore they could hear a new voice among them.

It was a girl's voice, and it too was calling for someone to follow.

Secret Enemies In The Hills

This story has been adapted from an original tale in Charles M. Skinner's book, Myths & Legends of our New Possessions & Protectorate, published by J. B. Lippincott Company, Philadelphia & London, 1900.

Long ago, in the golden lands of the Caribbean, where turquoise waves kiss pristine sandy shores and the emerald jungles whisper secrets to the wind, there lived a peaceful people known as the Siboney. They worshiped the great Spirit of the Sky, a being of kindness and light, who watched over their villages and guided the souls of the departed into the sacred caves of the hills. It was said that when one called out in the silent mountains and an unseen voice answered, and it was not an echo but a wandering soul speaking from beyond.

But peace never lasts forever. From across the great ocean, men clad in iron came, wielding fire and steel. They called themselves the Conquistadores, and with them came destruction. They tore through the villages like a hurricane, stealing, enslaving, and destroying all in their path. The Siboney fought bravely, but their wooden spears shattered against the invaders' armour, and their cries of defiance were drowned by the thunder of muskets.

Some fled deep into the jungles, vanishing like shadows among the trees, their voices lost to legend. Others hid in the sacred caves, where their spirits were said to linger long after death, whispering warnings to those who dared disturb them. Yet, not all of the oppressed bowed before the Conquistadores. In the mountains, hidden from prying eyes, the spirit of resistance still burned.

Among the scattered survivors were those who refused to be broken. They became the Guardian Brotherhood, warriors sworn to protect the land and its people from the tyranny of the Conquistadores. At night, they moved unseen through the jungle, striking swiftly like the panther before vanishing into the shadows. Some said they were ghosts, that the spirits of the Siboney had returned to seek vengeance. Others spoke of magic, of warriors who could summon the storms and command the beasts of the forest.

These hidden warriors were not alone. In the villages, beneath the watchful eyes of their oppressors, secret gatherings were held. Drums echoed in the night, their rhythms carrying messages to the hills. Dancers twirled in sacred circles, calling upon the spirits of their ancestors for guidance. Among them were the Mystics of the Moon, healers and seers who could read the future in the flicker of firelight and the rustling of the wind.

The Conquistadores, fearing the power of these hidden warriors, sought to stamp them out. They sent spies into the jungles, burned entire forests, and laid traps with gold and false promises. But the warriors of the hills were cunning. They struck at night, their faces painted like the spirits of the dead, their blades glinting like the fangs of the jaguar. They raided the Conquistadores' strongholds, stole back their captured kin, and left behind only the mark of the skull, a warning that vengeance was never far.

Yet, not all who fought the Conquistadores did so with honour. In the darkest corners of the island, a secret cult known as the Brotherhood of the Red Moon arose. Unlike the noble warriors of the hills, these men were driven by greed and vengeance alone. They danced in wild, frenzied rites, their bodies painted in eerie symbols, their chants summoning forces that even the bravest dared not speak of. Some said they could twist fate itself, cursing their enemies with incantations on the wind.

To join their ranks, one had to commit a terrible act, stealing the life of an innocent under the full moon, drinking their blood as proof of loyalty. Those who passed the test were marked with a brand upon their chest, the symbol of the Red Moon. The more they killed, the darker their mark became.

Even the Conquistadores feared them. At times, they struck deals with the Red Moon cult, setting them loose upon the villagers to sow fear and chaos. But the warriors of the hills had sworn an oath, to protect the innocent, no matter the cost. They hunted the Red Moon as fiercely as they did the Conquistadores, driving them further into the forbidden jungles.

One night, as the war raged on, the sea brought new warriors to the land. Sailors from the great ships of the north had arrived, seeking to challenge the rule of the Conquistadores. A great battle was waged, cannons thundering, swords clashing in the bloodied sands. Amidst the chaos, the warriors of the hills watched from the shadows, waiting for their moment.

It was then that a figure emerged from the mist, a tall man with silver hair, his face lined with the wisdom of years but his movements as swift as the wind. He carried no sword, no musket, only a single wooden staff carved with the symbols of the old spirits. Without a word, he led the warriors through the jungle, guiding them behind the Conquistadores' walls, where they struck with the fury of the storm.

By the time the sun rose, the battle was over. The Conquistadores had been driven back, their fortresses in flames. But when the warriors turned to thank the old man, he was gone. Some say he was a spirit sent by the ancestors, others that he was a forgotten king, come to reclaim his land before vanishing into legend.

Even now, when the night is still and the jungle breathes in whispers, some say he walks among the trees, waiting for the day the land calls upon him once more.

And so, the hills remain watchful, holding their secrets close, while the spirits of the past linger in the shadows, forever guarding the land of their ancestors.

The Legend Of The Bat Mountain

This story has been adapted from an original tale in Herman van Cappelle Jr's book, Myths and legends from the West Indies, published by Zutphen—Wj Thieme & Cie, in 1926. These tales were originally published in the Dutch language.

Long ago, when the moon still hung low and golden over the mountains of the Caribbean and the nights were thick with the scent of wild orchids, there lived a people called the Makoshi. They were forest folk, hunters, gatherers, weavers of hammocks and tellers of stories. They lived in small clusters of palm-thatched huts, nestled in valleys where parrots chattered and waterfalls sang like flutes.

But peace does not linger where fear takes root. One evening, just after the sun had slipped behind the sea and the shadows grew long and sharp, a strange wind passed through the trees. The dogs howled. The parrots fell silent. And from the highest peak of the darkened mountains came a sound unlike any other, a heavy fluttering, like the beating of giant wings.

Out of the sky swooped a monstrous bat, blacker than a moonless night and larger than any beast the Makoshi had ever seen. Its eyes gleamed like coals, its claws curved like sickles, and its wings blotted out the stars.

With a shriek that made even the bravest warriors clutch their spears, the creature descended into the village and snatched a man from outside his hut. Before a scream could rise, the bat had vanished, its victim gone with it, high into the hidden peaks of what came to be known as Bat Mountain.

From that night on, terror ruled the Makoshi. Each dusk brought dread, for as surely as the sun sank, the bat returned. Some nights it stole one. Others, it stole two or three. Warriors set traps, carved sacred totems, and painted their skin with river clay to confuse the monster, but it was clever. It left no tracks. It never returned to the same place twice.

The piaiman, the tribe's shaman, danced through smoke and flame, chanting to the spirits of the forest and sky. But the bat could not be banished. The people began to whisper that the creature was no mere beast, but a demon born of the underworld, a curse from the days when their ancestors first spilled blood upon the sacred soil.

Day by day, the Makoshi grew fewer. The fire circle where once they danced grew quiet. The hammocks swung empty. Children stopped laughing. Mothers stopped singing. It seemed the end had come, until an old woman named Ama rose from her hammock one twilight.

She was no warrior, no priestess, no leader. Her back was bent like a banana tree in storm season, and her hands shook like dry leaves. But her eyes were bright with something stronger than fear.

"I will go," she said. "I will give myself to the monster, so that we may know its path."

The villagers protested, but Ama only smiled. "I have danced enough, sung enough, lived enough. Let me give you one last story."

That evening, as the last gold light kissed the tops of the palms, Ama stood in the centre of the village. She wore her finest tapara beads, a cloak of woven vines, and beneath her shawl she hid a single fire-stick, a smouldering branch wrapped in dried sap and glowing ember.

The people watched from their huts, silent as stones, as the sky darkened and the wind shifted. Then came the sound, fluttering wings, heavy and slow. The bat fell from the sky like a storm cloud. Its talons wrapped around Ama, and with a scream that split the night, it soared back into the mountains, its monstrous wings casting flickering shadows on the treetops.

But Ama was not helpless. As the bat carried her into the dark peaks, she dropped bits of her fire-stick. Flames flared to life behind them, bright and terrible, like a comet streaking across the heavens. The fire marked the path they travelled, a trail of light in the black sky, pointing the way to the monster's lair.

The villagers saw the fire's trail and followed it. Through thickets and rivers, past jaguars and the cries of night birds, they climbed. And in the early hours, when the stars were fading and the sky turned grey, they reached a great stone ledge high atop Bat Mountain.

There, they found the nest of bones. It was a pit of horror. Bleached skulls and broken spears, torn hammocks and scattered beads lay scattered everywhere. At the centre of the nest, amidst ash and soot, Ama dropped the fire-stick and flames spread quickly. The monster's wings were ablaze, and it shrieked like a thousand storms as it twisted in the flame. Its great body collapsed, its wings curling inward like dried leaves.

And Ama? The stories differ. Some say the fire consumed her with the beast, and her spirit flew into the sky to watch over the Makoshi. Others say she escaped, burnt and battered, and wandered into the forest, never to be seen again.

But all agree on this: Bat Mountain still stands. And at its summit, there is a patch of scorched earth where nothing grows, a circle of stone white with ash and bone. No birds nest there. No beast climbs it. Only the wind howls through the rocks, and if you listen closely, some say you can still hear the fluttering of wings, and the whisper of an old woman's song.

And thus, the Makoshi were saved by the courage of one, and Ama the Flame-Bearer became a name passed from grandmother to child, a tale told by the fire when the night grows too quiet, and the bats fly too low. Even the smallest fire can burn away the darkest night.

Pretty Poll

This story has been adapted from an original tale in Walter Jekyll's book, Jamaican Song And Story, published by David Nutt, London,, in 1907.

Once upon a time, a Duke had a servant in his household. Now, this young woman had been courting a young man for quite some time. One day, another friend of the Duke came to visit. He saw the servant girl and instantly fell in love with her, and, as it happened, she fell in love with him too. So this gentleman asked the Duke for her hand. But the Duke shook his head and said, "No. She's already promised to another."

The gentleman was disappointed and left sadly.

Later, the servant went to the new man and said, "I love you. If you truly want to marry me, I'll leave my sweetheart and come to you instead."

"But how will you manage that?" the man asked. "The Duke won't allow it."

The young woman replied, "You just wait and see."

That very evening, when her original lover came to visit, she smiled sweetly and said, "Let's go for a walk, I want to show you something beautiful."

She already knew of a deep well out in a lonely spot, and she had a wicked plan. When they reached the place, she pointed into the well and said, "Look, what pretty flowers down there!"

As the young man leaned over to admire them, she shoved him hard into the well. He never came back up. The she clapped her hands together and said, "Thank God! Now I can be with the man I really love."

But up in the trees, unseen by her, sat a clever old parrot named Pretty Poll. He had watched the whole thing, and he flapped his wings and sang out:

"Ha ha! Ha ha!

I've got news for the Duke at home,

You pushed your dearest lover down into the well!"

The young woman looked up and saw the parrot, and her heart filled with fear. "Come down, Pretty Poll!" she cried. "Come here, lovely bird! There's a house made of gold and silver waiting for you, don't sit up in that old tree!"

But Poll just fluffed his feathers and sang back:

"A tree I was born,

A tree I must stay,

Until it's my time to fly away!"

And with that, he flew off, tree to tree, the young woman chasing after him and pleading all the way.

Poll flew through the forest, into the next village, then house to house until he reached the Duke's own rooftop. There, he perched and began to sing his song once more. The Duke heard the commotion and sent out his men. They listened carefully to what the bird was singing, and when they realised the truth of it, they seized the servant, brought her before the Duke, and had her punished. Her head was cut off for the crime she had done.

And as for Pretty Poll? He was taken in by the Duke, given the finest fruits and a golden perch, and was cared for lovingly ever after.

Anansi, White-Belly And Fish.

This story has been adapted from an original tale in Martha Warren Beckwith's book, Jamaica Anansi Stories, published by The American Folk-Lore Society, New York, in 1924. This story is as told by Mrs. Ramtalli, Maggoty.

There once lived a cunning spider named Anansi, who was known throughout the land for his wit, mischief, and insatiable appetite. Every morning, he would stretch himself out in the sun, lazy as you like, watching the birds soar overhead on their way to feed in the tall trees by the riverbank.

One fine morning, as the birds passed by, Anansi turned to his neighbour, a sleek bird called White-Belly, and said, "Brother White-Belly, where do you go to eat every day? Why not take me with you for once?"

White-Belly, wary but kind-hearted, gave him a sideways look. "Alright, Anansi," he said. "But only if you behave yourself. No tricks, no trouble."

"I swear on my eight legs," said Anansi, grinning.

So White-Belly, being the generous soul he was, fashioned a pair of wings for Anansi, false wings, of course, made from palm leaves and string. With a bit of help, Anansi strapped them on, flapped about a bit, and before long the two were soaring towards the feeding trees by the river. But Anansi, true to form, immediately began causing trouble.

Each time they landed on a new tree laden with fruit, Anansi would scurry forward and cry, "This one's mine! I saw it first!", and White-Belly, not wanting to quarrel, would flap away to the next. On and on it went, until Anansi had stuffed himself full to bursting. Belly round as a gourd, he found a branch in the sun and promptly drifted into a snoring sleep.

White-Belly had had quite enough. Quietly, he fluttered over, untied Anansi's fake wings, and took them away. The wind shifted, the tree swayed, and with a startled grunt, Anansi rolled off the branch and plunged straight into the river below.

Splash!

The river folk, the Fish, were curious creatures. They watched this strange, scraggly spider sink through the water and gently guided him to the riverbed.

"Who are you?" asked the eldest of them.

"Cousin Fish!" Anansi cried, dripping and desperate. "Don't eat me, please, we're family, after all!"

"Family?" The fish narrowed their eyes. "We'll soon see about that."

They brought forth a steaming pot of hot rice porridge, rice-pop, as they called it.

"If you're truly one of us," said the Fish elder, "you'll drink this down."

Anansi sniffed the pot and hissed, "No, no! It's not hot enough. Let's leave it in the sun to warm up properly!"

But what Anansi was really waiting for was for the porridge to cool. When the heat had faded, he slurped it all down greedily, not stopping until the pot was licked clean.

"Ah," said the elder. "Perhaps you are our cousin after all!"

Night crept over the river, and the Fish offered Anansi a place to stay. "There's a barrel of eggs in the kitchen," said the matriarch. "Mind yourself and sleep well."

But Anansi had other plans. He asked sweetly, "Would you be so kind as to let me sleep in the kitchen? I like the warmth of the fire."

Permission granted, Anansi waited until all the Fish were asleep. Then he tiptoed to the barrel of eggs and began poaching them, one by one, in the ashes of the fire. Each egg gave a soft pop! as it cooked and cracked. Only one egg was left by the time a small fish-child stirred and whispered, "What's that stranger doing in there?"

"Hush, child!" said the Fish mother. "Show some manners! He's our cousin now, let him rest in peace."

Morning came. The Fish mother sent her little ones to fetch the eggs for breakfast. But Anansi intercepted them. "No need to trouble the children," he said with a smile. "I'll do it."

He picked up the lone remaining egg, carried it to the mother, and presented it with a bow. She counted it, made a mark, but when she looked away, Anansi quickly wiped it off and returned the same egg again.

Over and over he did this, fooling her into believing that every egg in the barrel had been accounted for. By the time he was finished, the single egg had been marked a hundred times, and the others were long in Anansi's belly.

After breakfast, Anansi stretched and yawned. "Well, Cousin," he said, "it's been lovely, but I must be on my way."

The Fish, ever polite, called to her sons. "Take the canoe, my dears, and row our cousin across the river."

So the two Fish boys set off with Anansi in the boat. But the wind had turned sour, and the sky was beginning to darken with rain. Halfway across, a voice rose up from the shore.

"BRING THE STRANGER BACK HERE!" bellowed the Fish mother. "He's eaten all the eggs, only one is left!"

The boys looked at each other, unsure. "What did she say?" one asked.

Anansi waved his hand and replied, "She said, 'Row faster! There's a squall coming!'"

The boys obeyed and paddled harder. When they reached the other side, Anansi sprang from the boat, snatched up the young Fish, stuffed them into his sack, and scurried home. That night, he feasted.

And from that day to this, the people say that fish are for eating, because Anansi, with his silver tongue and greedy belly, was the first to ever taste them.

The Duppy

I've collected versions of this tale from various online and paper sources and this story is my own telling of the legend of The Duppy. The Duppy is most strongly associated with Jamaica, but it is also a significant part of folklore in Barbados, Trinidad and Tobago, the Bahamas, and other Caribbean islands.

Long ago, in a village nestled between the great green hills and the rolling sea, there lived a boy named Micah. He was a lively child, known for his quick feet and quicker tongue, always eager to chase after adventure. But Micah was also stubborn, and he scoffed at the warnings of the village elders, who spoke in hushed tones about the spirits of the night, the Duppies.

"Duppies are just stories to frighten children," he would say, laughing as he ran past the old cotton tree where spirits were said to linger.

One evening, as the sun melted into the horizon and the sky burned crimson, Micah ventured out beyond the village, past the yam fields and into the shadowed woods. He had heard of an abandoned house, crumbling with age, where no villager dared to go. They said it was cursed, that the spirit of a wicked man who had wronged too many still roamed within. But Micah, driven by bravado, wanted to prove he was not afraid.

As he stepped into the broken doorway, the air inside was thick with the scent of damp earth and something bitter, something old. The wooden floor creaked beneath his weight. A wind, though the air outside was still, whispered through the ruined walls.

Then, he heard a voice, soft as silk, but twisted into a tight knot of evil. "You shouldn't have come."

Micah spun around, his heart a drum in his chest. In the dim light, a figure moved in the corner of the room. It was a man, or what had once been a man. His skin was pale as moonlight, his eyes hollow, his grin too wide, too sharp.

Micah's heart slammed against his ribs as he ran, his breath coming in ragged gasps. His bare feet pounded against the wooden planks of the rickety house, splinters stabbing into his soles, but he didn't dare stop. The thing's voice still echoed in his head, smooth and taunting, the weight of its words pressing against his skull like a vice.

"You do not believe in Duppies… But that's no matter, for we most definitely believe in you."

The village was just ahead, its dim lanterns flickering through the thick night air. Safety. Familiarity. He pushed harder, lungs burning, legs screaming, the dense jungle swallowing the narrow path behind him.

But something followed.

The air grew thick, heavy, and just plain wrong. The scent of damp earth and rotting leaves was replaced by something putrid, like flesh left too long in the sun. The once-familiar night now stretched wide, too silent, too vast, the air pressing in around him like unseen hands. Groping at his skin. He stumbled onto the first dirt road of the village, barely able to keep himself upright. His grandmother's house was just ahead, its wooden shutters closed, its lantern burning faintly in the window. He reached the steps, slamming his fist against the door.

"Granny! Granny, open up!"

The door creaked open, but no warm arms pulled him inside. No worried voice chided him for making noise so late at night. The house was dark. Too dark.

Micah hesitated on the threshold, his breath catching. His grandmother never left the house unlit, not after sundown. The oil lamp on the table, the candles by the window, there was always something glowing, something to keep the shadows at bay.

But tonight, the darkness had claimed it all. A chill curled down his spine, cold fingers dragging along his skin. The warmth of the island night was gone. The air that seeped from the house was as cold as a graveyard breeze.

Then, in the farthest corner of the room, something moved. There was a figure, tall, gaunt, and swathed in shadows. Its limbs were too long, its joints bending at sickening angles. Its fingers twitched, slow and deliberate, curling like spider legs as it took a single step forward.

Micah's legs refused to move.

"You ran fast," the thing said, its voice a low rasp, thick with amusement. "But not fast enough."

The shadows behind it shifted, shapes writhing and pressing against the walls. Faces appeared, twisted, hollow-eyed, their mouths moving without sound. Some looked familiar. Some looked impossibly ancient.

They were Duppies.

Micah's throat tightened. His grandmother had told him the stories, had warned him of the spirits who walked after dark, who whispered in the trees and waited for those who did not believe. He had laughed at them, but now, he could only tremble.

The figure tilted its head, the movement unnatural, its grin stretching too wide. It knew. "You do not believe in Duppies," it repeated, its voice now everywhere, behind him, above him, beneath the floorboards. The walls seemed to breathe with it. "But that's no matter…"

The light from the lantern by the window flickered once, and then went out.

"…For we most definitely believe in you."

The door slammed shut. The darkness swallowed him whole.

The next morning Micah awoke with a start. The remnants of a dream, no, a memory, clung to his consciousness like damp linen. The house beyond the yam fields. The whispering voices. The unseen hands that had caressed his skin with a coldness unlike any breeze he had ever felt. He sat up, his breath shallow, his skin slick with sweat despite the cool morning air that crept through the wooden slats of his window.

And then he saw them. Footprints. Not his own. The dirt beneath his window was disturbed by small, bare feet, imprinted in the dust as though a child had been standing there.

Micah swallowed hard, his hands trembling as he pushed himself out of bed and crept toward the window. The prints led away from the house, winding through the yard, fading toward the fields. He wanted to tell himself it was a trick of the light, a figment of his imagination. But he knew better. The Duppy had found him.

From that day forward, Micah was never the same. His laughter, once as bright as the sun on the banana leaves, faded into a silence that unsettled even the oldest of the village folk. He no longer joined in the nightly domino games by the rum shop or whistled along to the calypso tunes that drifted through the streets. Instead, he kept to himself, shoulders hunched as though warding off an unseen presence.

His eyes were always searching. Even in the broad light of day, they flicked to the shadows beneath the trees, the dark corners of rooms, the empty spaces where no one should stand. When he walked the dirt roads home, he glanced over his shoulder, flinching at every rustling leaf, at every whisper of wind that sounded just a little too much like a voice.

People noticed. The old women shook their heads knowingly, muttering to one another as he passed. "Something followed him back." The men, though they said nothing, cast uneasy glances at him, their hands forming quiet signs of protection when his back was turned.

And Micah knew the truth in their fears. At night, when the world was silent and sleep should have come, he felt it watching him. The atmosphere in the room shifted, the air turning thick, pressing against his skin like a humid breath. Sometimes, the floorboards creaked when nothing moved. Sometimes, the whispering voices returned, curling around his ears like mist, calling his name in a tone that was neither man nor woman, neither near nor far.

One night, he made the mistake of looking. The candle by his bedside had burned low, the flickering flame casting long, distorted shadows on the wall. But one shadow did not belong there. A creature stood in the far corner of the room, tall and thin, its head tilted at an unnatural angle. Its limbs, too long, too still, seemed not fully formed, shifting with the candlelight as though struggling to decide on a shape.

And then, ever so slowly, it began to move. A single step. A second step. The floor did not creak beneath its weight. The air grew colder, and Micah's breath turned to mist before his face. He wanted to scream, to run, to wake himself from whatever nightmare had taken root in his home. But he could do nothing. His body refused to obey him, his limbs locked in place as the shadow crept closer, until the outlines of fingers, too many fingers, were mere inches from his face.

Then, just as suddenly as it had come, it was gone. The candle sputtered out. Darkness swallowed the room. And in the silence, a child's laughter echoed, distant, yet impossibly close.

Micah never spoke of what had happened in the house beyond the yam fields. But he knew, deep in his marrow, that once a Duppy had found you, it never truly let you go.

Obeah Witches

This story has been adapted from an original tale in Charles M. Skinner's book, Myths & Legends of our New Possessions & Protectorate, published by J. B. Lippincott Company, Philadelphia & London, 1900.

Long ago, when the Caribbean was still wild and filled with secrets, the islands were home to many strange and powerful beings. The winds carried rumours of mermen singing in the deep waters, spirits lurking in the shadows of the jungle, and witches who could bend the forces of nature to their will. Travelers feared the Jumbie, the restless spirit that roamed the night, and the Duppy, the ghost of the wronged. But none were more feared than the Obeah witches, who knew the ways of ancient magic and could summon powers darker than the stormy seas.

Among these, one such witch was known above all others, and she was called Old Nana Malva. She lived deep in the hills, where the trees grew so thick that no sunlight could break through. Her home was a hut made of bones and vines, and at night, the glow of blue flames could be seen dancing around it. They said she had a familiar, a great black beast with burning red eyes, that could change its shape, sometimes a hound, sometimes a shadow, sometimes a breath of wind.

Down in the valley, a young girl named Winyan lived with her cruel aunt. Winyan had no mother or father, only her two brothers who worked as fishermen. She dreamed of escaping her aunt's beatings, but she had nowhere to go.

One day, her aunt, who was rumoured to be an Obeah woman herself, said, "I have no more use for you, child. You must leave." And just like that, Winyan was cast out with nothing but the clothes on her back.

She wandered to the edge of the jungle and sat upon a great stone, singing softly to herself, her voice carried by the breeze. The night was falling fast, and strange sounds crept through the trees. Suddenly, there was a rustling in the brush, and out of the darkness came a creature, a massive, black hound with glowing yellow eyes. It was Old Nana Malva's familiar, the beast called Nyri.

"Come, girl," the hound spoke in a voice like thunder. "Come serve my mistress, or I will tear you apart."

Winyan trembled but did not run. Instead, she sang louder, hoping that her brothers might hear her. The hound bared its double row of dagger-like teeth and growled, but v stood her ground.

"You may take me, but I will never serve your dark mistress."

Nyri leaped forward, but at that moment, Winyan's brothers burst from the jungle, their spears gleaming in the moonlight. They had followed her song, and now they stood ready to fight. The hound snarled, its shadow stretching long like a creeping curse.

One of Winyan's brothers whispered, "We must be careful. This is no ordinary beast."

Winyan, thinking quickly, reached into her pocket and pulled out a small pouch her grandmother had once given her, a pouch filled with salt and sacred herbs. She flung it into the air, and as the grains of salt fell upon Nyri's dark fur, the beast let out an unearthly howl. Its body shuddered and twisted, shrinking into a black mist before vanishing into the trees.

Knowing they had little time before Old Nana Malva sent more of her minions, the three siblings ran. They reached their home just before dawn, and as the sun rose, they heard a scream in the distance, the cry of the Obeah witch, furious that her servant had been defeated.

But Nana Malva was not one to forgive. That very night, she sent a new terror, a three-footed horse, its eye a burning ember in the middle of its forehead. The villagers hid as its hooves pounded against the dirt roads, bringing doom wherever it stopped. Those who dared to look into its blazing eye were frozen in place, their souls sucked into the abyss.

But Winyan knew how to fight back. She had heard stories of this monster from the village elders, and she knew its weakness, Obeah magic could only harm those who feared it. So when the horse appeared outside her home, she stepped forward, heart steady, and spoke boldly, "You have no power here. Go back to the darkness."

The creature hesitated, its flaming eye flickering. It could sense no fear in Winyan's heart. With a terrible screech, it reared back and galloped away, its cursed form fading into the night.

From that day forward, the people of the valley knew Winyan was protected by greater forces than Obeah magic. And though the witches of the hills still cast their curses on the wind, none dared to touch her again, for even the darkest magic fears those with a heart full of light.

Bina, The Revived Father, And Isabella

This story has been adapted from an original tale in Herman van Cappelle Jr's book, Myths and legends from the West Indies, published by Zutphen—Wj Thieme & Cie, in 1926. These tales were originally published in the Dutch language.

Long ago, in the lands of winding rivers and ceiba trees, there was a Warrau village nestled near the mangrove's edge, where the waters sang old songs and the spirits watched in silence. There lived in that village a man named Taito, his wife Isabela, their two bright-eyed children, and Isabela's brother, a brooding and idle man whom the villagers called Bina.

Taito was a fisherman, a hunter, and a man of steady hands and an honest heart. Every day he worked hard to provide for his family. But Bina, though given a place under Taito's roof and food from his fire, did little but lounge in the hammock and chew cane all day.

One dawn, Taito rose with the dew and said to his wife, "Let's tend the orchard before the sun climbs too high. Brother, catch us fish for the pot. We'll return by midday."

But when they came back, they found no fish, no kindling, not even a fresh cut of cassava. Worse yet, the last of the salted fish from yesterday had been eaten.

Taito's brow darkened like a storm. "Must I hunt, plant, and fish while you lie like driftwood?" he snapped. "Fine then. I'll do it all myself."

He grabbed his harpoon-lance and went to the creek, his shoulders tight with anger.

Now Bina, stung by the words and twisted with envy, waited a moment, then followed Taito in his own canoe, his machete sharpened and gleaming by his side.

By the time Bina reached the creek, Taito had speared a fat silver fish and was tying it to the side of his canoe.

"Eh, you back already?" Bina called.

"I've caught enough for supper," Taito said, lifting the fish proudly.

"Let me see that spear," Bina said smoothly. "Maybe I'll catch one even bigger."

Taito, not suspecting foul play, passed the lance. As the two canoes drifted close, Bina stood and swung his machete in a flash, once, twice, and Taito slumped over, his blood staining the water red.

Bina tried to shove the body into the creek, but he was not as alone as he thought. Isabela, sensing danger that morning, had followed the trail with her two children, fearing what her brother might do. Just as Bina lifted Taito's body from his canoe, she stepped from the trees.

"No," she cried. "You will not toss him like rubbish! If you have killed him, then carry him home and bury him properly."

Startled, Bina obeyed. He paddled back with Taito's body, and under his sister's watchful gaze, he felled a tree and began to carve out a wooden coffin.

Isabela, meanwhile, sent her children to fetch their uncle, Taito's younger brother, and their grandmother. "Tell them not to be afraid," she said. "But tell them to come quickly."

Soon, the brother and old mother arrived. When they saw Taito's lifeless form and Bina digging a grave beside the hut, the brother burned with rage. But the old mother raised her hand. "Wait. Let the widow speak first."

Isabela stood beside the grave, a machete tucked beneath her skirt. When the coffin was ready, she had Bina place Taito's body inside, dressed in his best clothes, with his fishing knife and hooks beside him. As Bina shovelled earth over the grave, Isabela stepped behind him and, like a swift wave rising, struck him in the neck. He fell into the grave he had dug with his own hands. She buried him without clothes, without offerings, and without a prayer.

That same day, the old mother returned to her village with Taito's children and Isabela in tow. The family welcomed the grieving widow and her sons. But in this new home, the children were restless. They missed their father and each day, after eating, they would slip away to his grave, sitting in the shade and whispering to the soil.

On the third day, they met a strange little man standing by the edge of the trees. His skin was the colour of bark, his hair tangled like vines.

"Do you wish to see your father again?" he asked in a voice like wind rustling cane.

"Yes," the children said, wide-eyed.

"Then find the leaf of the guhuba tree," he said. "Rub it gently over the grave and return by afternoon. Your father will rise."

"But we do not know the guhuba tree," they confessed.

The little man plucked a few shining green leaves and showed them. "Tomorrow morning, do this. Come back after the sun has crossed the sky."

And so they did. The next day, with the hush of the dawn still thick around them, the boys went to the grave, rubbed the leaves as instructed, and returned home. That afternoon, they found a man waiting in the hut, sitting cross-legged, his voice soft but clear:

"Bring me water," he said. "I am thirsty."

The boys ran, brought him a calabash full, and once he drank, he asked: "Where is your mother?"

When he heard she was still with his mother and brother, he said, "Go get her."

The boys raced back and cried, "Mama, Papa is calling you!"

Isabela trembled. "Don't speak nonsense. He is gone."

But they pulled her hand and begged, and though she left her hammock behind, doubting still, she went with them.

When she arrived, her heart stopped, for there he was. Her husband. Whole and breathing.

"Where is your brother?" he asked.

"I buried him beside you," she said. "You will not see him again."

Taito nodded. "That is well."

Though weak at first, he regained his strength in the week that followed, cared for gently by Isabela. The villagers came to hear the tale, shaking their heads in wonder. Some say it was the tree-spirit Heboe who lent the power, while others whisper that Taito's soul had lingered out of love, refusing to pass on.

And Bina, the bad one, was never named in song or story again. But the people still say, "If you bury a good man, he may yet return. But bury a wicked one, and may he stay buried."

Cow And Anansi

This story has been adapted from an original tale in Walter Jekyll's book, Jamaican Song And Story, published by David Nutt, London,, in 1907.

One morning, Anansi was strolling near a cow pasture when he noticed something strange: all the cows were standing around, chewing on sticks and cleaning their teeth.

This made Anansi very nervous. He didn't trust cows one bit, especially not when they were all together doing something odd like that. So instead of going into the pasture, he climbed up into a tree at the edge and called out, "Howdy, Cow! Howdy!"

But none of the cows replied.

Now Anansi was even more frightened. He thought to himself, "Maybe if I offer them something sweet, like sugar cane, and pretend it's my chewstick, they'll be friendly with me."

That night, once the cows had left the pasture to graze elsewhere, Anansi hurried to fill his satchel with fresh cane. When he returned, the cows were still gone, so he climbed back up into the tree and slept there until morning.

As the sun began to rise, the cows returned. They stood beneath the tree, chewing cud and cleaning their teeth with their chewsticks. Then suddenly, a big chunk of something fell from the tree, right onto the ground in front of Papa Cow. Papa Cow looked up and saw Anansi perched in the branches.

"What are you doing up there?" Papa Cow called.

Anansi replied, "Oh, I've brought you a special chewstick!"

Papa Cow picked up the sugar cane and started chewing it. But instead of cleaning his teeth, he found himself swallowing all the sweet juice and the pulp as well.

"Mmm!" said Papa Cow. "This is delicious! Have you got any more?"

"Of course," Anansi said with a grin, and climbed down from the tree.

He handed out bits of sugar cane to all the cows, telling them it was his own special kind of chewstick. Then he pulled out a bottle filled with sweet cane juice and asked Papa Cow if he wanted a sip. Papa Cow took one sip, then another, and before long he had drunk the whole bottle.

The cows were thrilled. "Anansi," they said, "you're alright!"

And just like that, Anansi became friends with the cows.

Later, Anansi invited Papa Cow to visit his home. "Come by," he said. "I'll show you where I get my magic chewstick from."

But Papa Cow hesitated. "Don't you have people at your house? I'd be embarrassed if they saw me."

"No, no," Anansi lied. "There's no one home. But just to be safe, I'll go ahead and tell anyone there to leave before you come."

Anansi rushed home and warned his family and neighbours, "I'm bringing Cow back with me. Don't make any noise or you'll scare him off."

But they weren't happy. "If you bring Cow here, Anansi, we'll never trust you again!"

Anansi waved them off. "Just keep quiet," he said, and grabbed a rope before heading back.

When he returned, he told Cow, "See? No one's at my house. Come along, let's go."

As they set off, Anansi added, "You're such a shy fellow, Brother Cow. Just in case the children see you and start shouting, let me tie this rope gently around your neck. That way, if you get scared and try to run, I can keep you steady."

Cow agreed, and they carried on.

"Now listen," Anansi said, "if you hear the children making noise when we get close, don't be frightened. Just wag your tail to show you're brave."

As they approached the yard, Anansi called out, "Look here, my friends, my special guest is coming! Say hello to my friend!"

He turned to Cow and said, "Wag your tail, don't worry about them."

When they reached Anansi's house, he stopped under a large tree at the front. "Brother Cow, wait here," Anansi said. "I'll go inside first and prepare the place. My wife doesn't know I'm bringing a visitor, so I can't just walk you in."

But Anansi wasn't going to prepare a welcome, he was going to sharpen his tools. He planned to kill Cow and feast on him. He left his eldest son outside to keep an eye on Cow, but Anansi didn't trust the boy to keep quiet, so he kept popping back to check. Each time he came out, he shouted, "Wag your tail, Cow! Don't be afraid!"

Eventually, when the sharpening was nearly done, Anansi came back out and saw Cow still calmly wagging his tail. "What's this now?" Anansi snapped. "Didn't I tell you not to wag your tail in my yard?"

Cow, bothered by flies, just kept wagging.

Anansi turned to one of the villagers and said, "See that? This fellow's got the nerve to make my children cry with his ugly face!"

Then he stepped close to Cow and warned, "If you don't stop wagging that tail, something's going to happen."

But Cow didn't stop. The flies were still bothering him, and he just kept swatting them away. So Anansi raised his machete and swung at Cow's neck. But Cow jerked his head back just in time, the blade sliced through the rope instead, and Cow broke free. He took off like a shot, running as fast as he could back to the pasture.

"Come back, Brother Cow!" Anansi shouted. "It was only a joke, just a little fun!"

But Cow didn't stop running. He ran all the way home and never looked back. From that day forward, Anansi could never go near a cow again. And anytime a cow saw him, they'd chase him off with their hooves and horns. And that is why you'll never see Anansi hanging around cows.

Why Tumble-Bug Rolls In The Dung

This story has been adapted from an original tale in Martha Warren Beckwith's book, Jamaica Anansi Stories, published by The American Folk-Lore Society, New York, in 1924. This story is as told by William Forbes, Dry River, Cock-pit country.

Once, in a time when the world was still young and full of trickery and wonder, there lived two creatures in the warm hills of Cockpit Country, Mr Anansi, the infamous spider known for his cunning ways, and Tumble-bug, a humble dung beetle with a good heart but not much sense for deception.

Word spread far and wide that the king of the land had a beautiful daughter, radiant as the moon and graceful as the breeze, and he had made a bold declaration. "Whoever brings me a jar filled with money, honest money, shall have my daughter's hand in marriage," the king proclaimed.

Naturally, this caught the attention of every eligible creature, but none were so eager as Tumble-bug and Anansi.

Tumble-bug, despite his simple ways, was diligent and earnest. He scuttled through the forest and fields, working hard, and after many days, he managed to fill a fine jar with real coins, with shiny, proper money that gleamed in the sun.

Anansi, however, as clever as he was lazy, had no such luck. He couldn't be bothered with the effort of gathering money. Instead, he did what he knew best, he plotted. Finding an empty jar just like Tumble-bug's, he filled it not with gold or silver, but with cow dung and horse droppings. He packed it all in neatly, put a lid on it, and chuckled to himself. "This will do," he said. "This will do just fine."

On the day they were to present their jars to the king, Anansi and Tumble-bug travelled together, each with their jar tucked beneath their arms. As they neared the palace, they came upon a small roadside shop. Anansi, always thinking ahead, put on his most charming voice.

"Brother Tumble-bug," he said, "Let's stop for a drink, eh? We've a long walk ahead of us. A little something to wet the throat would do us good."

Tumble-bug, being polite and agreeable, nodded eagerly. "Alright, Anansi. But let's make it quick."

They stepped into the shop, and as Anansi paid for the drinks, he also picked up a loaf of bread. "You wait here," he said slyly. "I'll fetch the bread."

But outside, with no one watching, he did a wicked thing. He swapped his dung-filled jar with Tumble-bug's jar of money. The jars looked nearly identical, and Tumble-bug, trusting as ever, never thought to check.

They finished their drinks, and with the jars in hand, continued on their way to the palace. When they arrived, the king stood at the head of the courtyard, his daughter beside him, veiled in silk. An audience had gathered to witness the suitors' offerings.

"Let the first man step forward!" the king called.

Anansi, grinning from ear to ear, stepped up and placed the jar, Tumble-bug's jar of money, on the clean white sheet laid out before the royal court. With a dramatic flair, he opened the lid and turned the jar over. Out tumbled coins, bright, beautiful coins! The crowd gasped and cheered.

"A fine gift!" the king declared. "This one may court my daughter!"

Tumble-bug, still unsuspecting, stepped forward proudly with the jar Anansi had left him. He bowed deeply and lifted the lid with great ceremony. But as he turned it over, there was no jingle of coins, only a soft plop, plop as cow dung and horse droppings splattered across the white sheet.

The crowd recoiled in horror. The princess pinched her nose. The king leapt from his throne. "What foulness is this?!" he bellowed.

Anansi, ever the actor, pointed in mock outrage. "Look at this disgrace! Look what this nasty fellow has brought into the royal court! Dung! Filth! Take it away, take it away!"

The guards shoved poor Tumble-bug aside as the crowd laughed and jeered. His little heart broke from shame. He had done nothing wrong, but there he was, humiliated in front of all.

From that day forward, Tumble-bug was never seen without his ball of dung. He rolled it everywhere he went, pushing it diligently across fields and roads, not because he loved it, but because he was always searching, searching for the truth, searching for justice. Some say he still believes that if he rolls long enough, he might find that jar of money again. And that, children, is why to this day, the dung beetle rolls in filth.

The Virgin's Diamond

This story has been adapted from an original tale in Charles M. Skinner's book, Myths & Legends of our New Possessions & Protectorate, published by J. B. Lippincott Company, Philadelphia & London, 1900.

Long ago, in the golden age of the Caribbean, there lived a young soldier named Miguel José. He was kind-hearted and dutiful, but though he served bravely in the city of Havana, his family back home in a small island village was growing poorer by the day. Each letter he received from his aging parents was filled with desperate pleas, first for food, then for medicine, then for a new roof to keep out the stormy rains.

Miguel's heart ached, but his wages were meagre, and the paymaster claimed that no gold had arrived for months. His comrades were as poor as he, and army rules forbade him from earning money outside his duties. He could neither borrow nor beg, and so, one evening, heavy with sorrow, he wandered beyond the barracks and into a quiet chapel, kneeling before the statue of the Virgin Mary.

"Oh Holy Mother," he whispered, his voice trembling with desperation. "You, too, know the pain of seeing a loved one suffer. Please, I beg you, help my mother in her time of need."

No answer came amid the flicker of candlelight in the silence of the church. Yet, something within him told him to return the next night, and the night after that.

On the third evening, as Miguel knelt with fresh tears wetting his cheeks, something astonishing happened. The air turned warm and sweet, like the scent of island blossoms, and when he lifted his head, he gasped, for the glass eyes of the Virgin's statue had filled with tears, and they rolled down her carved cheeks. He barely had time to marvel before, with a rustle like silk, the statue moved.

The Virgin stepped down from her pedestal, her expression tender, full of understanding. Without a word, she extended her hand toward him, and there, upon her delicate finger, gleamed the most famous treasure in all of Havana, the Virgin's Diamond, placed there years ago by a devoted nobleman.

Miguel's breath caught in his throat. Surely, she did not mean…

But she smiled and nodded.

With shaking hands, he took the jewel, pressing a reverent kiss to her fingers before she returned to her place of honour, as still and silent as before.

Miguel ran from the chapel with his heart pounding in his chest. There was a man in the city, Señor Hyman Izaaks, a discreet lender who helped those in need, though some said that he asked for too much in return. Miguel hurried to his door and, with the diamond trembling in his hands, he secured more money than he had ever dreamed possible. That very night, he sent the gold home, his heart swelling with relief.

But the next morning, the church was in an uproar, for the Virgin's Diamond was gone! Priests, bishops, and even the governor's men scoured the city, questioning everyone. It wasn't long before someone recalled seeing Miguel enter the chapel the night before, so he was promptly arrested and dragged before a military tribunal.

To their astonishment, Miguel made no effort to hide the truth. "I did not steal," he declared proudly. "The Holy Mother herself gave me the diamond, out of mercy for my suffering family."

The judges discussed this among themselves. If he was a common thief, he deserved the harshest punishment. But if he spoke the truth, then who were they to defy the will of the Virgin? If they punished him, would they not be inviting divine wrath upon themselves?

At last, the council reached a peculiar verdict. They seized the diamond from Señor Izaaks, without bothering to repay him, much to his dismay, and returned it to the Virgin's hand.

As for Miguel? He was declared "Not guilty… but told firmly not to do it again."

Though he was spared, Miguel was left with nothing, for the money was already on a ship bound for his family. But he smiled as he walked free, for he knew that somewhere, in a quiet village beneath the Caribbean sun, his mother's prayers had been answered. And perhaps, just perhaps, the Virgin herself was smiling down upon him.

The Happiness Jar

This story has been adapted from an original tale in Herman van Cappelle Jr's book, Myths and legends from the West Indies, published by Zutphen—Wj Thieme & Cie, in 1926. These tales were originally published in the Dutch language.

Long ago, in the deep green belly of the forest, where the mahogany trees grow tall and the parrots chatter like old gossips, there lived a man named Bako. He had a small thatch-roof hut near the edge of the woods, a quiet wife who cooked with care, and two sons with eyes as sharp as any mongoose and hearts full of questions.

Now Bako was not a bad man. He worked hard when he had to, hunted and fished as all men did, and came home each day with his basket, even if it was only filled with forest roots and stories. But Bako had one weakness, he loved good food more than anything else in the world. Not just food to fill the belly, no, he craved the kind of meals that made the mouth sing and the eyes roll back in the head.

One afternoon, as he was returning home through the bush with little more than twigs and a squirrel to show for his hunting, Bako caught the smell of something rich and savory. It curled through the air like incense, sweet, smoky, and thick with spices. He followed it until he came upon an old banab hut, half-sunken into the earth, with vines coiled around its posts like lazy snakes. It looked abandoned, forgotten, but from within came the sound of something gently bubbling over fire.

And inside, there sat a pot. The fire beneath it was glowing red, and the lid rattled like it had secrets to spill. Just as Bako stepped inside, the pot stopped bubbling, and then, to his amazement, it spoke.

"You hungry, man?" it asked, with a voice like coconut milk poured over hot stones.

Bako nearly fell over. "Hungry? Starvin'!" he said, holding his belly with both hands.

"Then sit your tail down," said the Pot. "I got just the thing."

With a hiss and a sizzle, the pot filled the air with the smell of roasted bird. In moments, out floated the most tender, juicy drumstick Bako had ever seen, seasoned with herbs no one could name and sauce as thick as sugar cane molasses.

Bako ate until he couldn't breathe, then leaned back against the banab wall, smiling like a man who had caught the moon. "Thank you, Pot," he said, and the Pot replied, "Come back anytime."

From that day on, Bako visited the banab every chance he got.

When he came home, his wife would lay out cassava cakes or grilled fish, and he would wave them away. "No, woman. I ain't got no appetite. My belly's full."

At first she thought nothing of it. But days passed, and still he came home refusing food. Meanwhile, she noticed the little pile of smoked fish and stored cassava was shrinking fast. She begged him to go out and shoot a few morokot birds for the stew pot, and he agreed, but never brought any home. Instead, he slipped away to the forest and let the magical Pot do the feeding.

The two sons, clever boys that they were, noticed everything. They whispered to each other in the shadows.

"How come Papa eat nothing, but he look fat like he full?"

"You think he feeding by the spirit folk?"

"Nah. He up to something. Let's follow him."

So one day, they tracked Bako into the bush. They watched from behind a clump of ferns as he entered the banab and bowed before the talking Pot. The Pot, as usual, offered up roasted meats and peppered stews, and Bako gobbled it up without a word for anyone but himself.

The boys waited until he left and crept into the hut. The Pot sat glowing, content. "Hungry?" it asked.

They grinned. "You bet."

The Pot fed them too, sweet mango-glazed pigeon, smoked boar belly, even wild yam curry. The boys cleaned every drop, and being raised with good manners, they scrubbed the Pot clean until not even the ghost of a scent remained.

When Bako returned later, licking his lips and eager for more, he sat before the Pot and asked as usual, "Fix me something good, friend."

But the Pot sat cold. Silent.

Bako asked again. "Please, I haven't eaten all day."

Nothing.

He reached out and gave the side of the Pot a tap. "You deaf now?"

Finally, the Pot let out a puff of cold smoke. "You greedy man," it said, in a voice no longer warm but sharp like a splinter. "You take and take, and never give. Not a crumb for your wife, not a bone for your boys. You thought happiness was yours to hoard, but joy is like food, meant to be shared."

Bako dropped to his knees. "I didn't mean to! I just… "

"You just got fat on kindness you didn't earn," said the Pot. "And now, I'll cook no more. Not for you, not for anyone."

And with that, the fire went out. The Pot cracked clean down the middle with a sound like a thunderclap, and the forest fell silent.

Bako returned home with a heavy heart and an empty belly. He found his wife had cooked a simple stew from what little was left, and this time, he ate in silence, shame heavy on his tongue.

He never told her what he'd done, but the boys knew, and they never let him forget. And though Bako still roamed the forest, he never again found the banab. Some say the vines grew thick and swallowed it whole. Others believe the Pot moved on, waiting in some hidden glade for a better soul to feed.

But old folks say this, "If you ever smell pepper stew in the middle of nowhere and hear a voice whisper, 'You hungry?', think twice before you answer."

For the Happiness Jar gives only to those who know that joy, like food, must never be eaten alone.

John Crow And Fowl-Hawk – Part 1

This story has been adapted from an original tale in Walter Jekyll's book, Jamaican Song And Story, published by David Nutt, London,, in 1907.

One day, Fowl-Hawk came to visit John Crow and said, "Come take a walk with me, brother. There's a place I know, dangerous, yes, but there's something there I was promised."

He continued, "I passed a river once and met Fowl there. Fowl was struggling, so I helped him up. He promised that when his chicks were born, I could come for one. Well now, the chicks are here, but when I went back, Fowl acted like he'd made no such promise. I tell you, brother, the chicks are plump and fresh, perfect for us to eat. And it's not just one, he's got a whole brood! We'll feast! But… the place is dangerous."

John Crow frowned. "I've heard bad things about that place," he said. "I don't think I want to go."

"You're a fool," said Fowl-Hawk. "We're men, aren't we? We'll be fine! If they try to catch us, we'll just fly off. Last time I went, I swooped right into Fowl's yard. We argued the whole day, and I'm still alive, aren't I? Come now, good friend, let's go."

So off they flew. They flew high and far, until they reached the land where the chicks were. Fowl-Hawk called out, "Brother John! We're here! Look down there, so many fresh chicks!"

John Crow hovered uncertainly. "I don't want to go down there."

"You're being foolish," said Fowl-Hawk. "Just come a little lower."

They landed on a tree, and Hawk said, "See? You can spot them better from here. I'll sing so they know I'm coming."

John Crow said, "If they hear you, they might kill us!"

"Nonsense," said Hawk. "Fowl and I are friends. We only had a little quarrel."

Then Hawk sang out loud:

"Here I come, I'm on my way!

I'm coming for what was promised,

Twillinky twing ping ya, I'm on my way!"

Fowl heard the singing and quickly told his chicks to hide. Dog was a hunter and a good friend of Fowl, Fowl always treated him kindly. So Fowl ran to Dog and said, "Danger's coming! Fowl-Hawk's on his way to take my daughter. Please come to my yard and shoot him for me."

Dog agreed and went with Fowl to lie in wait.

Meanwhile, Hawk turned to John Crow again. "Let's go down now."

John Crow said, "No."

"You'll starve if you stay up here."

"I'll wait for what God gives me," said John Crow.

Fowl-Hawk scoffed. "Wait for God? You'll get nothing that way. Look at me, I go after what I want. And I'll tell you this, if I do get anything, I won't share a single bit with you! Fool!" And with that, Fowl-Hawk started singing again as he descended:

"Here I come, twillinky twing ping ya..."

John Crow And Fowl-Hawk – Part 2

This story has been adapted from an original tale in Walter Jekyll's book, Jamaican Song And Story, published by David Nutt, London,, in 1907.

…but just as Fowl-Hawk landed, BAM!, Dog fired his gun. Fowl-Hawk was dead.

John Crow burst out laughing. "Ha-ha! Let me put on my dusty old coat and go see what happened to that fool."

He flew down and, finding Fowl-Hawk's body lifeless, said, "Thank God! Ha-ha!"

He plucked out Fowl-Hawk's eyes. "These are the eyes he used to see his doom coming," he said, and popped them in his pocket. Then he started feasting on the body.

Dog looked over and said to Fowl, "That's sorted then. Sister, if they ever come again, just send for me. I'd stay longer, but I'm furious. Yesterday I sent my son out with money to give to Brother Monkey. But who did he run into? That wicked Puss! Beat my boy, stole the money, and told him he had a grudge against me. Since he can't beat me, he'll take it out on my children. So I've got to go. There'll be blue fire when I catch that Puss!"

Dog stormed off to Puss's house and shouted from the gate. "Puss! I want water and a bit of fire!"

Puss sneered. "Get away from my gate. I know why you're here."

Dog growled, "Ah, me man, there'll be blue fire!"

But Puss's gate was locked, he had company that day. Rabbit was visiting.

"I want to see you!" Dog shouted.

Puss replied, "Go away, your mouth's long like a devil's fork!"

Dog broke the gate and stormed in, but Puss locked himself inside and shouted insults through the window until Dog had no choice but to leave.

Later, Monkey said he'd go get the money from Puss, after all, they were good friends.

So Dog went home, fuming, and from that day on, he held a grudge against Puss that lasted until the end of his days.

Hunter, Guinea-Hen And Fish

This story has been adapted from an original tale in Martha Warren Beckwith's book, Jamaica Anansi Stories, published by The American Folk-Lore Society, New York, in 1924. This story is as told by Thomas Williams, Harmony Hall, Cock-pit country.

Once upon a time, in a quiet corner of the Cockpit Country where the forests rolled like waves across the land, there lived an old hunter who had spent most of his days roaming the hills in search of game. One day, while wandering farther than usual, he stumbled upon a most splendid piece of land. The soil was dark and rich, the kind that promised bountiful harvests.

"Well now," the old man said to himself, rubbing his beard with satisfaction, "this land is too good to leave wild. I'll make it my own and plant peas and corn."

And with that, he set to work that very day, cutting back the bush and clearing the ground. But what he didn't know was that the patch of land he'd found wasn't just any bit of wilderness, it was the feeding ground of Miss Guinea-Hen, a clever creature known to dwell in the shadows and keep to herself, only coming out at night to forage.

When Guinea-Hen saw the clearing the old man had made, she clucked with glee. "Oh, look how kind the master is! Clearing my field so I can feed better. Let me lend a claw and tidy up a bit myself!"

And so, while the old man slept, she scratched at the earth and did a bit of her own clearing. The next morning, the old man returned and was surprised to see the land even cleaner than he had left it.

"Well, bless me soul," he muttered. "I must've done more work than I thought yesterday." And feeling encouraged, he chopped more bush and started preparing the ground.

That night, Guinea-Hen came again. "More work? He's really going all out for me! This must be fate. Let me finish off what he left."

And again, she cleaned and cleared, scratching up the last of the brush.

By the third day, the old man burned all the cuttings. Guinea-Hen, coming upon the smoking field that evening, flapped her wings in delight. "Oh, he even burned it for me! What a fine friend. I must make good use of this place."

The old man, still thinking he was doing all the work, planted peas and corn that very day. That night, Guinea-Hen returned and pecked away at the freshly planted seeds.

"Why should I plant my own when he's already done the hard part?" she chirped. "I'll just help myself."

Every day, the old man returned to find more of his crops eaten or missing.

"What pest is doing this?" he grumbled. "Some insects, maybe?"

Still, he replanted, determined to reap a harvest. But no matter how many times he planted, Guinea-Hen feasted each night, and the crops never stood a chance.

Weeks passed, and soon the remaining peas and corn began to ripen. The old man rubbed his hands together and said aloud, "Tomorrow, I'll harvest what's left."

But Guinea-Hen heard him from her perch in the trees. "He's coming for it tomorrow? Oh no, not before I get my share!"

That night, she took a trip down to the sea and called out to her old friend, Fish, using her leaf-trombone to sound a strange, watery tune across the waves. Fish swam up and listened as Guinea-Hen told him her plan.

"I've a field full of ripe corn and peas, but the old man plans to take it tomorrow. I need help gathering it tonight."

Fish nodded.

"I'd love to help, but I can't walk, and my fins won't carry me far. You've wings and legs, why don't you lend me one?"

Guinea-Hen thought for a moment.

"I can't spare my legs, but I'll lend you my wings. See that straight road? You can fly and drop, fly and drop. I'll run on foot and meet you there."

So Fish strapped on the wings, and off they went, one gliding through the air in bursts, the other dashing along the forest paths. They met at the edge of the field and began gobbling up the old man's harvest under the cover of night.

But just before dawn, when the sky began to glow, Guinea-Hen paused and kept looking around nervously.

"What are you peeking about for?" asked Fish.

"Oh, just keeping an eye on that butterfly over there," Guinea-Hen lied. "Let me borrow back my wings, I'll catch it for you."

Fish, ever trusting, handed them over. Guinea-Hen fastened them quickly, flapped once, twice, and vanished into the sky. Moments later, the old man arrived. He gasped at the destruction, half his crop gone, the rest scattered. He muttered to himself as he bent to salvage what he could. Then, as he reached down to pull up a stubborn root, he saw something strange beneath it, a shimmer, a flicker, Fish! The poor creature, flopping and trembling, had buried himself beneath the plants, but the wings were gone, and now he could neither swim nor fly.

"Well," said the old man. "It's you who's been ruining my crops?"

Fish, fearing for his life, pleaded, "No, not me! I'm innocent! Please don't kill me, I'll sing for you instead!"

Now the old man, who had a soft spot for music, agreed. "Very well, but sing something good."

He filled a tub with water, placed Fish inside, and listened as the creature began his song:

"She man yerry me bra, hey!

She man yerry me bra!

Guinea, guinea, quot amba tory!"

The rhythm was strange and catchy. The old man began to sway, then shuffle, then twirl, dancing with delight.

"Take me to the seaside," Fish said between verses, "and I'll sing even louder!"

The old man, caught in the spell of the tune, hoisted the tub onto his head and danced all the way to the sea. Fish sang, the waves lapped, and the music grew stronger. Then, just as a large wave rolled in, Fish gave one mighty flick of his tail and leapt into the swell, gone in an instant, carried home by the sea.

The old man spun and stomped, still caught in the rhythm. Only when the song had ended did he look into the tub and find it empty.

"Gone?!"

He ran home, grabbed his hook and line, and rushed back to the shoreline, casting again and again, hoping to catch the trickster Fish.

And that, children, is why we still fish at sea today. For the clever Fish never came back, and the Guinea-Hen? Well, she never lent her wings again.

The legend Of La Diablesse

I've collected versions of this tale from various online and paper sources and this story is my own telling of the legend of The legend of La Diablesse. The legend of La Diablesse is most associated with Trinidad and Tobago, but versions of this folklore also exist in Saint Lucia, Dominica, Grenada, and Haiti.

This night in the village was thick with heat and the scent of damp earth, but Jean did not feel it. His mind was lost to the haze of rum and the lingering thrill of the evening's revelry. The sound of laughter still echoed in his ears as he stumbled along the narrow path home, his feet unsteady, his senses dulled. Then, he saw her.

She stood beneath the crooked old tamarind tree, bathed in the pale glow of the moon. Her dress, flowing and as white as bone, clung to her slender frame, and a wide-brimmed hat tilted over her face, hiding all but the barest glimpse of her lips, which were red, like a fresh wound. A soft, floral scent drifted toward him, something sweet and wild, like orchids left to rot.

Jean stopped in his tracks, his breath catching in his throat. She was stunning, more beautiful than any woman he had ever seen. His pulse quickened. Who was she? Why was she here, alone in the night?

"You're lost, aren't you?" Her voice was velvet, a whisper against the hush of the trees.

Jean swallowed hard, suddenly aware of the dense silence pressing in around him. The village was behind him, far behind. He hadn't realized how deep he had wandered into the forest's edge.

Jean had been warned. The old men at the rum shop, their eyes clouded by age and memory, had muttered her name between sips of dark liquor. The women at the river, wringing clothes beneath the moonlight, had whispered cautionary tales of men who had wandered off into the night, never to be seen again. Even the children, usually so reckless and wild, dared not speak too loudly of her, lest she hear them and come looking. Deep in their cups, the old timers said that she preyed on men and men alone.

The woman stepped forward, her movements fluid and unnatural, too smooth, like water flowing uphill. The dim moonlight shimmered against her dress, the fabric impossibly clean despite the thick mud and tangled roots beneath their feet.

"Come," she murmured, stretching out a delicate hand, her voice as soft as silk and as cold as the grave. "I'll take you where you need to go."

Something inside him twisted, a primal warning clawing its way up his spine, screaming at him to turn and run. But his body was no longer his own. His legs moved forward against his will, his fingers twitching at his sides as if trying to break free of invisible threads pulling him toward her.

The path beneath their feet grew wild and overgrown, the tree roots gnarled like the fingers of the dead, their twisted forms seeming to pulse beneath the soil. The air thickened, the night sounds fading one by one, swallowed by a creeping silence. There were no insects, no rustling leaves, no chorus of frogs by the river, only the soft undertone of her skirts dragging over the earth and the distant crash of waves against unseen rocks.

Jean's throat was dry. His heart hammered against his ribs. Something was wrong. "Where are we going?" he asked, his voice barely more than a whisper.

She stopped. Slowly, she turned to face him. The wide-brimmed hat, always low over her face, slipped back just enough to reveal what lay beneath. Jean had expected beauty. Instead, his breath left him in a shuddering gasp.

Her face, or what was left of it, was a ruined thing, a grotesque parody of life. Her skin, stretched taut over her bones, was mottled with decay, blackened lips peeling away from jagged, yellowed teeth. Her mouth twitched, twisting into something that was neither a smile nor a snarl, but a hungry thing.

Her eyes were empty pits, fathomless black voids that burned with something ancient, something patient. She had waited a long time for him.

The scent of damp earth thickened, turning sour, turning rotten. Jean stumbled back, his mind finally wrenching itself free from her spell. Horror clawed at his throat. He turned, trying to flee, but the forest had changed. The trees had closed in, their trunks pressed together like the bars of a cage. The path he had walked was gone, replaced by tangled undergrowth that shuddered and twisted as if breathing. His feet slipped on loose, crumbling earth, the ground shifting beneath him as if something beneath it was stirring, hungry and waiting.

Behind him, she laughed. Low. Knowing. The sound curled through the air like smoke, settling into his lungs, wrapping itself around his heart. The ground beneath him gave way. Jean fell, his scream swallowed by the waiting dark. The last thing he saw was her, standing at the edge of the abyss, smiling down at him with that awful, peeling grin.

The sea raged against the jagged cliffs of the island's northern shore, the waves churning as though they, too, recoiled from the horror that lay at the base of the precipice. Jean's body was broken, his limbs twisted at unnatural angles, his face stretched into by rictus into an expression of unspeakable terror. His unseeing eyes were locked wide open, as if even in death, they still beheld the nightmare that had lured him to his doom.

The villagers found him at dawn, when the scent of salt and decay drifted through the humid air, leading the search party to the rocky abyss where he had plummeted. Some of the men gasped, others turned away, bile rising in their throats at the grotesque spectacle.

But none of them were surprised. They knew. Jean had been taken by La Diablesse.

The story spread like wildfire through the village, reaching every home, slipping into every heart like a slow poison. They crossed themselves when they spoke his name. No one wanted to claim his body. No one wanted to bring a cursed man back into their village. Because once La Diablesse marked you, the grave was the only escape.

Why King Congo Was Late

This story has been adapted from an original tale in Charles M. Skinner's book, Myths & Legends of our New Possessions & Protectorate, published by J. B. Lippincott Company, Philadelphia & London, 1900.

In the old town of Santiago de Cuba, where the warm air was thick with the scent of sea salt and crushed sugarcane, the people prepared for their most peculiar and lively celebration. All Kings' Day was a grand event, a day when slaves and freedmen alike took to the streets in parades of wild colours, their laughter and music echoing between the stone buildings. And at the head of it all, as always, was King Congo.

No one knew his true name anymore. Some said he had been born a slave, while others swore he was the lost son of an African king. He wore his title like a badge of defiance, strutting through the town in a ragged captain-general's hat, a faded lieutenant's coat, and a single epaulette that had seen better days. On his feet, he wore nothing at all, yet he demanded spurs for his mule. To the people of Santiago, he was a legend, a clown, and a king all at once.

That year, the parade was to be the grandest yet. The drums had been tuned, the tambourines jingled, and the fine ladies wrapped themselves in bright new bandanas. The Spanish officers and the town clergy stood waiting in the square, ready to observe the spectacle. But as the hour struck and the parade gathered, there was one problem, King Congo was missing.

At first, the people laughed. A king must make his subjects wait, after all! But as the sun climbed higher and still there was no sign of him, unease settled over the crowd. Where was he?

A group of his loyal followers set out to search the town. They checked the old rum shops, the shade of the mango trees, and even the church steps where he sometimes napped after too much aguardiente. But there was no sign of him. Then, at last, a frightened boy ran up from the lower streets, breathless.

"They took him," the child whispered. "The ones from the hills."

A silence fell.

'The ones from the hills' was a phrase whispered only when absolutely necessary. The people of Santiago knew well the stories of those who lived deep in the jungle, beyond the sugar fields and coffee plantations. There were shadows that watched from the trees, and figures that lurked behind the mist. Some said they were spirits, remnants of the lost Siboney people, waiting for revenge. Others claimed they were escaped slaves who had sworn blood oaths to the gods of the old lands. None dared to go near them.

But King Congo was not afraid of spirits or oaths. And that, perhaps, had been his mistake. That morning, just before dawn, he had been seen strutting through the lower streets, boasting to all who would listen that he had discovered a precious thing hidden in the caves beyond the town. A gift from the spirits, he had claimed, meant for a true king. Had he gone to the hills to take it?

The search party hesitated. But with the festival ruined and the crowd growing restless, they had no choice but to go after him. Armed with machetes and torches, they ventured beyond the edge of town, into the thick jungle where the vines curled like serpents and unseen creatures rustled in the undergrowth.

After an hour of searching, they found his mule. The poor creature stood trembling beneath a ceiba tree, its eyes rolling in fear. But there was no sign of King Congo. Only a single boot, lying in the grass.

A cry came from the bushes. One of the searchers had found something else, a trail of footsteps leading to a dark cave in the hillside. At its mouth, the air was thick with a strange, coppery smell. And there, lying just inside the entrance, was King Congo's uniform, the captain-general's hat, the lieutenant's coat, the faded blue breeches. All neatly arranged. But no body. Only a deep, dark tunnel, descending into the earth.

The searchers did not wait to see what lay beyond. They turned and ran, back to the town, where they spread the terrible news. Some swore that King Congo had been taken by the spirits of the Siboney, who had dragged him into the underworld. Others believed he had stolen something cursed and been swallowed by the jungle itself.

But the elders of the city, the ones who knew the old ways, spoke of another truth. King Congo had called himself a king. But a real king had been sleeping in those hills, watching and waiting. And when a man takes what is meant for the true king, then the true king comes to seek payment.

From that day on, no one ever ventured near the caves again. And the next year, when All Kings' Day arrived, there was no King Congo to lead the parade, for the spirits had chosen a new king, and he ruled in silence, beneath the hills.

Black Tiger, Wau-Oeta And The Broken Bow

This story has been adapted from an original tale in Herman van Cappelle Jr's book, Myths and legends from the West Indies, published by Zutphen—Wj Thieme & Cie, in 1926. These tales were originally published in the Dutch language.

In the time before the old trees forgot how to whisper and the rivers still sang songs of memory, there lived a man in a village carved from the green heart of the Caribbean jungle. He was not a great man, nor one who boasted riches or skill, but he was kind, and he worked hard, even if fortune never followed him home.

He had two brothers-in-law, both proud hunters, men of sharp arrows and louder mouths. Each evening, they returned from the forest with meat hung over their shoulders, wild pig, deer, or turkey, and laughter that echoed through the village like drums at a feast. The unfortunate man brought home only silence, and for this, they mocked him quietly, then cruelly, and finally with hatred.

One day, the brothers-in-law came to him and said, "Let us all hunt together, brother. There is a place deep in the forest where the game is rich and plentiful."

The man's heart swelled with hope. "Truly?" he asked.

"Truly," they lied.

And so, at dawn, the three entered the emerald maze of the jungle. But once they had journeyed far from the village, the brothers spoke again. "Let us split up. You go east, we shall go west. When the sun begins to fall, we shall meet beneath the great silk-cotton tree by the river."

They smiled as they spoke, but the smile was as thin as a snake's hiss, for the path they had given him led not to any hunting ground, but to the lair of the dread beast, Tobe-Horoanna, the Black Tiger of the forest, a shadow in fur, a monster whispered of in firelight tales.

The man wandered along, growing uneasy, until he stumbled upon a wide path beaten into the earth. "Where am I going?" he muttered aloud. His question was answered by the sudden crash of underbrush and the earthshaking growl of the Black Tiger.

The beast leapt from the trees, black as pitch, teeth like jagged white roots, and eyes burning as red as coals. The man turned and fled, racing for the thickest tree he could find. Round and round the trunk they ran, beast chasing man, man dodging death, until the man, seeing no escape, dared to try a trick. He reversed direction suddenly, leaping behind the tiger, and with a sharpened flint he had used to gut fish, he slashed the beast's hind legs.

The tiger collapsed with a roar, unable to stand. The man took his only arrow, notched it into the bow he had carved as a boy, and loosed it into the creature's neck. The tiger writhed. With trembling hands, the man then drove his knife deep into the tiger's chest. The Black Tiger shuddered once more, and died.

When the man returned to the village, he was spattered in blood and carrying the tiger's pelt over his shoulders like a cloak. His brothers-in-law, who had not gone to the meeting place at all, turned pale when they saw him.

"You are alive?" they said, feigning joy. "We feared you had been lost."

But the man only smiled and said, "I found a beast in the jungle, and now the jungle will speak my name."

The old chief did not believe his tale until the man led them to the place where the tiger's body lay, stiff and cold. The villagers whispered and made signs against evil.

"No man kills Tobe-Horoanna," they said. "He is a spirit, not a beast."

But when the man danced atop the tiger's body and cried, "See? Dead, dead, dead!" the old chief stepped forward, clapped him on the shoulder, and said, "Today, you have two wives."

He was given another daughter, and his brothers-in-law, now full of shame and jealousy, built him a fine new hut. They called him Ai-ja'mo, headman and hero, and the drums sang of his name.

But the man felt uneasy. He had killed a monster, yes, but what if his luck did not last? What if he returned to being the forgotten brother, the empty-handed one? So he went to find Wau-Oeta, the Rain-Frog spirit, keeper of secrets and luck, who lived in the hollow of a tree said to touch the clouds.

He journeyed deep into the jungle until he found Wau-Oeta's tree. There, he sat beneath its wide roots and cried to her. "Wau-Oeta!

Help me! I wish to remain lucky in the hunt. I beg you, grant me your blessing."

No answer came.

Night fell. Still he cried. Still he pleaded.

Then came a rustling, a rustling not of wind, but of procession. One by one, the forest came alive. A parade of birds walked before him. The tiny Doroquara, who pecked at his toes, was followed by parrot, toucan, owl, and hawk, all tapping his foot with their beaks. Then came the rats, the Acouri, the Labba, the deer, the bush pigs, even the majestic tapir. Each licked his foot with their tongue. Then came the tigers, small ones, then great ones, followed by the snakes, who flicked their tongues across his skin and coiled silently away.

At last, when the dawn split the trees with light, Wau-Oeta appeared. She was neither woman nor beast, but something in between, a spirit with moss on her skin and moonlight in her eyes.

"You made a great noise," she croaked. "You disturbed my rest."

"I am sorry," said the man. "But I needed your help."

"Then look at your arms."

He did, and to his horror, he saw they were covered in a pale, soft mould.

"That fungus has clung to you like sorrow," she said. "It spoils your luck. Rub it away, and let me give you what you came for."

She held out a strange arrow, broken into pieces, each piece split again, but humming with power. "Take this," she said, "but tell no one where it came from, or it will vanish forever."

The man returned home and found that his bow now sang with every shot. When he loosed Wau-Oeta's arrow, it disappeared into the air, yet each time it struck down a bird, a rat, a deer, a pig, a tiger, even a serpent. In the order they had greeted him, so did they fall. He returned from every hunt with meat enough for a village. His fame spread across the island and people came from faraway coasts to see him.

But his brothers-in-law still burned with envy. And so, when the great Paiwarri festival came, when the fermented cassava drink flowed like rivers, they brought him cup after cup. At last, drunk and proud, he let his secret slip. He told them of Wau-Oeta, of the tree, the mould, and the arrow that never missed.

They laughed, and he laughed with them. But when morning came and the drums were silent, he reached for the magic arrow, and found only his old one, cracked and dull. His luck had vanished.

The forest grew quiet around his hut. His wives wept, for the game was gone. The people no longer sang his name. His brothers-in-law hunted with broad smiles.

And sometimes, when the rain falls softly and the frogs sing at dusk, a man can be seen sitting at the base of a tall tree in the jungle, weeping softly, calling out to a spirit who will never answer again, for Wau-Oeta gives once, but never twice.

And the arrow that never missed now lies somewhere deep in the earth, broken again, waiting for another man brave enough, and wise enough, not to speak.

Hog And Dog

This story has been adapted from an original tale in Walter Jekyll's book, Jamaican Song And Story, published by David Nutt, London,, in 1907.

Once upon a time, there was a hog named Cuddy. One day, Cuddy went out in search of a job. He walked all over the place, asking here and there, but no one had any work for him. When he finally returned home, he was met by Ratta, who offered him a job.

"Cuddy," said Ratta, "I need someone to keep watch for me in case Brother Cat comes sneaking around."

Cuddy asked, "And how much are you paying for that?"

Ratta replied, "I'll give you three shillings and sixpence a week, but you'll have to feed and water yourself."

Cuddy wasn't too pleased with that arrangement, but times were tough, and he needed the money. "All right," he sighed. "I'll manage until the end of the week."

At the end of the week, Ratta paid Cuddy his wages. But Ratta, thinking Cuddy was still on the job, went out again. When he returned, however, Cuddy was nowhere to be found.

"If it hadn't been for the grace of God," muttered Ratta, "Puss would've gotten in and had me for supper!"

Fuming, he cursed Cuddy. "May that hog wander forever, never finding work," he said. "And may others, worse off than him, laugh at his misfortune!"

The very next morning, Cuddy set off once more to look for work. Now, Dog, who worked as a market watchman, was sitting by the gate when he saw Cuddy pass by.

"Oi, Cuddy!" he called. "Where you off to?"

"I'm out looking for a bit of work," said Cuddy.

At that, Dog burst out laughing. "What, I thought you were working with Ratta?" he teased.

Cuddy felt so embarrassed, he didn't even reply. He just kept walking. But Dog wasn't done. He laughed and laughed, then began to sing:

Times are hard, when even Hog's jobless,

Dog's at the market, laughing at Hog's mess.

Rarabum Cuddy's at the door,

Rarabum Cuddy's at the door,

Rarabum, Cuddy's at the door!

Dog kept singing and laughing until Cuddy, fed up and humiliated, turned back and went home. And from that very day, Hog has hated Dog. And to this day, Hog cannot stand the sight of him.

Settling The Father's Debt

This story has been adapted from an original tale in Martha Warren Beckwith's book, Jamaica Anansi Stories, published by The American Folk-Lore Society, New York, in 1924. This story is as told by Simeon Falconer, Santa Cruz Mountains.

In the green folds of the Santa Cruz Mountains, where the sun rose lazily over the tamarind trees and the wind carried the scent of sugarcane, there lived a young boy named Eli. He was the youngest in a rather curious family known for their riddles and roundabout ways of speaking. His father, Mr. Joseph, was a quiet man with more debts than coins, and his sharpest tool was not his machete, but his wit.

One morning, a sharp knock echoed on the wooden door of their little house. Eli, no more than twelve, opened the door to find a well-dressed man standing there with an impatient look and a leather-bound notebook in hand.

"Good morning, young man," the man said briskly. "I'm looking for your father. He owes me five dollars."

Eli blinked. "Oh, my father's not here, sir. He's gone to break a new fence to mend a rotten one."

The man frowned. "And your mother?"

"She's gone to the market to sell sweet to buy sweet."

The visitor's brow twitched. "And your older brother?"

"Gone to sea to catch what in catching will kill, and what he doesn't catch, he'll carry home alive."

The man took a step back. "All right… And your sister?"

"She's inside the house, weeping over what she was rejoicing about last year."

The man stared at him. "And what about you, boy? What are you doing?"

"I'm takin' hot bricks out the oven," Eli said simply, brushing at his heel.

The man huffed. "Right, well, that's quite a list of puzzles you've just handed me. I tell you what, if you can explain all that nonsense, I'll give you five dollars myself."

Eli grinned. "Alright then.

He cleared his throat and stood a little straighter.

"When I said my father's gone to break a new fence to mend a rotten one, I meant he's gone to borrow five dollars from someone else to pay the five dollars he owes you."

The man's eyes narrowed, but he said nothing.

"When I said my mother's gone to sell sweet to buy sweet, I meant she's selling honey to buy sugar. Still sweet, just different kinds."

The man tilted his head. "Go on."

"When I said my brother's gone to sea to catch what in catching will kill, and what he don't catch he'll bring home alive, that means he's gone to bed to catch lice. The ones he catches, he'll kill. The ones he don't catch will stay in his head."

The man's face curled in disgust, but he couldn't help the grin twitching at the corners of his mouth.

"As for my sister," Eli continued, "last year she was over the moon to have her baby. Now she's weeping because the child's taken ill and might not make it."

A pause followed.

"And me? I said I was takin' hot bricks out of the oven, but really, I'm pulling chiggers out me feet. Burn like fire, they do."

The man let out a long breath and shook his head, laughing.

"Well, boy," he said, reaching into his pocket, "you've turned every riddle inside out and made them make sense. That's cleverer than most grown men I know."

He handed over a crisp five-dollar note and said, "Here. You've earned it."

Eli took the note with a nod. "Then please, sir, use it to settle my father's debt."

The man raised an eyebrow. "What, you don't want to keep it for yourself?"

"No, sir," Eli said. "A man must keep his word, and my father gave his."

The man smiled wide now. "A boy of riddles and honour. The world could use more like you."

And so, he pulled out his ledger, scribbled a receipt, and marked Mr. Joseph's debt as settled.

From that day forward, people spoke of the boy who paid off a grown man's debt with nothing but wisdom and wit. Some say he grew into a fine judge. Others claim he became a storyteller whose riddles could open locks. But all agreed on one thing: Eli had pulled something greater than chiggers from his heels that day. He'd pulled the whole family out of trouble. And he did it with words.

The Lusca

I've collected versions of this tale from various online and paper sources and this story is my own telling of the legend of The Lusca. The legend of The Lusca is most closely associated with The Bahamas, particularly around the blue holes found in the region. However, similar sea monster myths exist in other parts of the Caribbean, including Barbados, Haiti, and Jamaica.

The sea had always whispered to Idris. As a child, he had lain awake in his mother's small shack, listening to the waves rolling against the cliffs, murmuring stories older than time itself. His grandmother had warned him never to venture too close to the blue holes, those deep, endless abysses that punctuated the waters around the island.

"The Lusca waits there, boy," she had told him, her voice a raspy warning. "She's got a hunger bigger than the ocean itself. One minute, the water's still and as calm as glass, the next, it's boiling, and whatever's near gets pulled under. Gone."

Idris had laughed then, too young to believe in such things. But he wasn't laughing now. The sea was dead quiet. The only sound was the creaking of his fishing boat as it drifted near the gaping maw of the blue hole. The water, dark as ink, stretched beneath him like a wound in the world. He shouldn't have come this close. He should have listened.

Idris peered over the side of his fishing boat, his breath shallow. The water was too still, too deep. Something about it felt wrong. He had been fishing these waters his whole life, knew their rhythms and moods like a second language, but tonight, the sea had fallen silent. Not a ripple disturbed its surface, not a single fish stirred below.

Idris gripped the worn wooden oars of his small fishing boat, his knuckles pale against the dark night. The sea was calm, too calm. The water's surface was like a great sheet of black glass, barely rippling beneath the glow of his flickering lantern. He had been fishing these waters for years, but tonight, something felt wrong.

Then, a shadow moved. A massive, slithering shape glided deep beneath his boat. Not a shark. Not a barracuda. Something bigger. Much bigger.

Idris froze. He watched the creature's impossibly long silhouette stretch beyond the weak glow of his lantern, a monstrous shape that seemed to never end. The sea groaned, a low, resonant vibration that rumbled up from the abyss and shook the hull beneath him. The air grew thick, pressing in on his chest, making his every breath feel like it was being forced from him. His gut screamed at him to flee.

He scrambled for the oars, hands shaking, fingers fumbling uselessly against the smooth wood. Move. Row. Get away. But his body felt sluggish, as if the ocean was holding him there.

Then, the sea exploded. The water erupted with a deafening roar, and something enormous surged from the depths. A wall of churning black water crashed over him, slamming into the boat with the force of a hurricane. His lantern was swallowed by the waves, plunging everything into darkness save for the glaring white gleam of the moon. Tentacles, thick as tree trunks lashed through the air, their suckered surfaces glistening,. They did not move like normal things, not like eels, nor squid. They jerked unnaturally, writhing, snapping, searching.

Then Idris saw the Lusca. Its grotesque, pulsing body was neither octopus nor shark, but something caught between nightmares, something the ocean had kept hidden for centuries. The head was a writhing mass of tendrils, each one coiling and unfurling like hungry fingers. And beneath them, a gaping maw split open, ringed with rows of dagger-like teeth, endless, spiralling inward as if meant to consume everything.

Idris had no time to scream. A massive tentacle slammed down on the bow of his boat. Crack. Wood splintered beneath the impossible weight. The boat shuddered violently, tilting as water rushed into the widening cracks. He was going in. Then the world flipped. The boat snapped in two. Idris plunged into the water.

The cold stole his breath away, filling his mouth with salt water, burning his throat, his lungs. The ocean surged around him, under him, above him, a crushing force that dragged him into nothingness. His limbs flailed, desperate to find the surface, but there was no direction in the water, only depth.

The current shifted. A deep, vacuum-like pull yanked at his body, dragging him downward. The water began to spiral, forming a whirlpool around the blue hole beneath him. The Lusca was pulling him in. Idris thrashed wildly. His arms clawed at the water, his legs kicked, but it was like fighting against a hurricane, but it was o use, for the ocean owned him now.

A dark shape loomed below, twisting, waiting, patient. The thing's tentacles moved with horrifying precision, coiling in the water like vipers preparing to strike. Two burning orbs opened in the abyss, vast and endless, glowing like submerged embers. They locked onto him, searing through his soul, seeing everything he was, every fear, every moment of helplessness, every secret of his existence. He was nothing to this creature. Nothing.

The whirlpool's pull intensified, yanking his body downward. His chest ached, his lungs burning for air, but the ocean did not care. The tentacles moved. One lashed forward, striking through the water like a whip, wrapping around his ankle. The pressure was immense, crushing his bones, dragging him toward the gaping mouth below.

Idris fought. He kicked and tried to tear himself free, but there was no escape. The last thing he saw before the sea swallowed him whole was the Lusca's terrible mouth stretching open, endless and black, a void from which nothing had ever returned.

Then there was silence. The ocean surface smoothed over, calm once more.

The next morning, the villagers found the wreckage of Idris's boat washed up on the shore. The wood was shattered, the nets shredded, and the oars broken clean in two. But there was no sign of Idris.

The Voice In The Inn

This story has been adapted from an original tale in Charles M. Skinner's book, Myths & Legends of our New Possessions & Protectorate, published by J. B. Lippincott Company, Philadelphia & London, 1900.

The moon hung low over the Cuban countryside, casting long shadows along the old Minas road. The air was thick with mist, curling like ghostly fingers around the twisted trees. An old inn, long abandoned and sagging with decay, sat brooding in the darkness, its broken windows like hollow eyes staring into the night. It was here, in this cursed place, that the trial of a man accused of robbery had brought fear and dread to the court of Puerto Príncipe.

"Speak plainly, Señor. Say what you heard." The prosecuting attorney, Don Pablo Ramirez, twirled his pointed beard impatiently, his sharp gaze fixed on the witness. The tribunal watched with weary indifference, save for the elder judge, who kept glancing at the crucifix on the wall. When the sun touched the bleeding Christ, it would be time for lunch. But for now, the shadow still lingered.

The witness hesitated. "You will not believe me."

"Never mind your fears. You say you were passing the old inn when you heard a voice. Was it one of the brigands?"

"No, Señor. It was something… worse."

The court stirred uneasily. Even the accused, a ragged and sullen man, seemed to stiffen in his seat.

"Explain," the attorney demanded.

The witness swallowed hard, leaning forward as if afraid to be overheard. "It was not the voice of the living, Señor. It came from beneath the ground."

A shudder ran through the room. The judge crossed himself, his appetite momentarily forgotten.

"From beneath the ground? What did it say?"

The witness's voice dropped to a whisper. "It was a terrible moan, like a soul in torment. It said, 'For the sake of the Virgin, of Her Blessed Son, of the Holy Saint Peter, of the Good God, pray for me. Pray for a sinner. Beg the good fathers at Nuevitas to say a mass for the soul of Enrique Carillo.'"

The words hung in the air like a curse.

A gasp came from Don Pablo Ramirez. The prosecutor's face drained of colour, his lips trembled, and his hands shook as they clutched the edge of the table. The court erupted in murmurs.

The elder judge shot to his feet. "Clear the court! It is the fever!"

Panic seized the room. The onlookers scrambled for the doors, fleeing as though death itself had entered the chamber. Only the defence lawyer rushed to Ramirez's side, helping him into a chair. A glass of water was brought, which he drank in quick gulps.

"No, no," Ramirez croaked, waving a feeble hand. "It was nothing. A moment of weakness."

The trial hurried to its end. With no solid evidence, the accused was set free. Yet as he slunk from the courtroom, he cast a long, knowing glance at Ramirez.

That night, the air in Puerto Príncipe was thick with rumours. Some said that Don Pablo had taken ill, while others said he was haunted. But the worst rumours claimed that the voice from beneath the inn had called his name.

Two nights later, travellers were waylaid near the abandoned inn. One man disappeared without a trace, and fear spread like wildfire. That same evening, a lone figure left Don Pablo's house. A cloak drawn high around his face, he moved quickly through the darkened streets. His steps, though careful, did not go unnoticed.

"Señor Ramirez?"

The prosecutor froze. A tall man stepped from the shadows. "I am Captain Alfonso Garcia Estufa of the Engineer Corps. I come from Havana with orders to discuss the brigands troubling this province."

Ramirez hesitated, his face hidden in the folds of his cloak. Then he forced a smile. "Of course, Captain. My home is yours while I see to some business. Please, make yourself comfortable."

With that, he disappeared into the night.

In the morning, the captain and his men had vanished from Puerto Príncipe. No one knew where they had gone.

The next night, as the moon waned, two travellers rode along the Minas road, their horses trudging through the mud. Lantern light swung beneath their mounts' necks, casting eerie shapes along the path. As they neared the ruined inn, a low whistle sounded. The door burst open, and a group of armed men rushed forward. Torches flared, casting a crimson glow on wicked grins and gleaming knives.

One of the riders threw up his hands. "Take the money, take everything! Just spare my life!"

The second man, tall and cloaked, swung from his saddle. Calmly, he lifted the lantern, tilting his hat just enough to show the shadowed outline of his face. He rifled through his companion's belongings with an expert's touch, tossing aside anything of little value.

The brigands watched, awaiting orders. One among them, a man recently freed from prison, smirked. "Hurry, boss. Before someone hears."

Then, from the depths of the earth, a voice wailed, "For the sake of the Virgin, of Her Blessed Son, of the Holy Saint Peter, of the Good God, pray for me. Pray for a sinner. Beg the good fathers at Nuevitas to say a mass for the soul of Enrique Carillo."

The cloaked figure recoiled as if struck. His hands flew to his ears, a strangled groan escaping his lips. The torchlight flickered, illuminating the terror on his face.

Then came another voice. "As you value your lives, do not move."

Flames blazed to life around them. Soldiers emerged from the shadows, rifles raised, faces set in grim determination. At their head stood Captain Estufa.

"Fire!"

Two shots rang out. The cloaked figure stumbled, clutching his chest. He fell, his body sprawling across the road. The soldiers rushed forward, yanking away the fabric that shrouded his face. Don Pablo Ramirez lay dead, his lifeless eyes staring toward the inn.

Beneath the floorboards of the old inn, the remains of Enrique Carillo were found, along with the bones of many other victims. It was said Ramirez had lured them there, using the brigands as his pawns, growing fat on their stolen wealth.

But the dead do not rest easily. To this day, travellers who pass the ruined inn on All Souls' Eve claim to hear voices rising from the earth, whispering through the cracks in the stone.

"Pray for me."

And among them, louder than the rest, wails the voice of Don Pablo Ramirez.

The Legend Of Letterwoutstomp

This story has been adapted from an original tale in Herman van Cappelle Jr's book, Myths and legends from the West Indies, published by Zutphen—Wj Thieme & Cie, in 1926. These tales were originally published in the Dutch language.

Long, long ago, before the grandmothers of grandmothers were ever born, when the trees on the island still knew their old names, and the rivers sang with spirits, there was peace across the land. The Carib and Arawak peoples lived as one with the earth. The piaimen, the wise spirit men, kept watch over the balance between good and wickedness. The fish were fat in the creeks, the cassava sweet, and the forests thick with game. Smoke from the barbacot fires curled gently toward the stars, and the laughter of children echoed under the palm trees. But all things change.

One day, from beyond the rim of the sea, great floating beasts came, made of wood and roaring wind. From the belly of one of them stepped a man unlike any the islanders had ever seen. His skin was the colour of sun-bleached bone, and he moved stiffly, as if he had too many bones to fit inside his skin. And he had a mouth where no mouth should be. Not on his face, no, his face was smooth and cold. His mouth gaped from the middle of his chest, rimmed with yellow teeth like sharpened oyster shells. And it was always open. Always hungry.

They named him Paira-Oendé, but among the island tongues, he became known as Letterwoutstomp, 'The Mouth-on-His-Chest'. He brought steel and fire. He brought death. Where he walked, forests withered. Where he feasted, no songbird sang again.

Letterwoutstomp was no mere man. He hunted not for food, but for flesh. He ate men, women, and even the elders. He burned villages and laughed with that chest-mouth, that gaping hole that never stopped chewing. He spared no one. Not even children.

And when the people fled, he chased them on horseback and from ships, across sand, through mangrove, and into the hills. It was as if the spirit of hunger itself had taken form and was walking the land. The people wailed. They begged the piaimen to act, and so the piaimen called upon the spirits.

They drank the bitter paiwarri, burned the smoke herbs, and summoned the great serpent, the Double-Spirit of the earth and sky, whose coils wrapped around the world. The Snake Spirit listened, and the piaimen gave word to the people to retreat to the sacred tabbetje, the hidden spirit-mound hidden, where the songs of the ancestors still lingered on the wind.

There, for eight days, they vanished from the world. Not a single soul was seen in the villages. Not a fish-net tugged. Not a hammock swung. Letterwoutstomp grew furious. He searched, he cursed, but he could find no one to eat. The island had gone completely still. But that sort of stillness does not last.

Letterwoutstomp carved himself a great canoe, not from wood, but from the bones of a giant caiman, enchanted and cursed. With eyes of coal and jaws of stone, he rode the rivers like a demon of the flood. He sailed up the Marowijne, his monstrous boat gliding like a spectre toward the river called Kwaloe, where the people had gathered once more. He meant to devour them all in one great feast, to wash the land in blood.

But the piaimen had seen this coming. For nights, they danced by firelight, their chants curling up into the trees, calling again on the Serpent Spirit. They asked not for protection, but for vengeance. They asked that the beast be swallowed by a greater beast. And so the river stirred. As Letterwoutstomp caiman-vessel neared the shore, the waters rose. The sky darkened, though no cloud moved. From the deep, the Worgslang, the spirit-serpent of old, uncoiled. It rose up, and up, and up, its scales shimmering with lightning, its eyes the colour of dawn fire. It opened its jaws wide, and before Letterwoutstomp could cry out, the serpent swallowed him whole, man, mouth, caiman and all.

The monstrous boat was cast ashore by the force of the water, turning cold and heavy, then sinking into the earth. And there, to this very day, it lies, a stone caiman resting on a stone bank, seen by those who still know where to look.

That night, the island roared with celebration. The people danced. They sang to the stars. Feathers flew like birds, and the drums did not stop until sunrise. From every mouth, one chant rose:

"The serpent has eaten the eater."

At dawn, an elder piaiman, as grey as moon-bark and as thin as smoke, walked to the great stone face of Temere Rock, and with blade and fire, carved into its surface the tale.

He carved Letterwoutstomp. He carved the caiman. He carved the snake rising from the river. And when his work was done, he whispered a final blessing, saying, "Let this be remembered, when the sea brings mouths with teeth again." And to this day, those who remember sing:

In the basin of the Maroni River,

Where the jungle still holds breath,

Stands the stone of ancient battle,

Worn by time, but not by death.

Temere Rock sings in silence,

Marked by fang and fire and fight,

Where the serpent saved the island

And swallowed up the night.

Beware the mouth on chest, young ones,

If you see one near the bay,

For though the first was taken down,

Another walks the waves today.

Wheeler

This story has been adapted from an original tale in Walter Jekyll's book, Jamaican Song And Story, published by David Nutt, London,, in 1907.

One day, Brother Puss set out on a journey and walked until he came to the mouth of a wide river. Now, Puss was terribly afraid of water, so he couldn't cross. He ended up stuck there for two days and one night, perched in a tree that hung over the river.

Meanwhile, Mr Anansi was out fishing. He cast his line and fished his way along the river until he happened to come near the very tree where Puss was hiding. But Puss didn't say a word. As Anansi went on, he came upon a strange hollow stump by the riverbank. Curious, he tapped it gently. He tapped… and tapped… and tapped again, until he finally slid his hand inside.

Suddenly, something grabbed him from within! Anansi panicked. He pulled and pulled, but he couldn't free himself. Then he called out, "Who's holding me?"

And from the stump, a voice replied, "Me, Wheeler."

Anansi, thinking quickly, said, "Well then, Wheeler, wheel me a mile and a half!"

And in a flash, Wheeler spun him high through the air, hurling him a mile and a half away. When Anansi finally landed, though bruised and battered, he stood up, dusted himself off and said, "Thank goodness! I may have had a little accident, but I see this could be a good living for me and my family!"

So Anansi went back home, fetched some sturdy iron pegs, and returned to the spot where he had landed. There, he planted the pegs into the ground right at the spot, like sharp teeth waiting in the earth.

Up in the tree, Puss was watching everything.

Later, when Anansi had prepared his trap, he returned to the stump and waited quietly. Soon, Brother Peafowl came walking by.

"Brother Peafowl!" Anansi called out. "There's a fine opportunity for the both of us here!"

Peafowl, curious, asked, "What kind of opportunity?"

Anansi led him to the stump. "You see that hole? With your long, fine wings, just reach in, you'll find something grand."

Peafowl, ever the proud bird, thrust his wing in. Snap! Wheeler grabbed hold of him too!

"Try to pull away!" Anansi encouraged, hiding his glee.

Peafowl pulled with all his might, but couldn't break free.

Anansi grinned and said, "Ask now, 'Who's holding me?'"

Peafowl cried, "Who's holding me?"

The voice answered, "Me, Wheeler."

"Then tell him," said Anansi, "say: 'Wheel me a mile and a half!'"

And just like that, Peafowl was flung into the air, landing straight onto the iron peg. Anansi chuckled, picked him up, popped him in a sack, and returned to the bush to lie in wait again.

Up in the tree, Puss still watched.

Soon after, Brother Ratta came along. Anansi greeted him with a wide grin. "Ah, Brother Ratta! Just the decent gentleman I love to see."

Ratta raised a brow. "Oh? Why's that?"

"Don't be afraid," said Anansi. "There's an opportunity here for you and me both!"

He took Ratta to the stump and said, "See that hole there? Put your hand in, you'll find something good."

Ratta, suspicious but tempted, reached inside. Snap! Wheeler had him too.

Ratta panicked. "I'm stuck!"

Anansi said, "Ask who's holding you."

"Who's holding me?"

"Me, Wheeler."

"Well then," Anansi instructed, grinning, "say: 'Wheel me a mile and a half!'"

Once again, Wheeler flung Ratta through the sky, smack onto the iron peg. Anansi added Ratta to the sack and settled back again.

Now, clever old Puss decided it was time. He climbed down from the tree, wandered a little through the bush, and then returned to the river looking meek and mild, pretending he had no clue what was going on.

Anansi, delighted to see him, called out: "Brother Puss! Come and see this wonderful thing I've found! A real living for both of us!"

Puss played dumb and walked slowly over.

Anansi eagerly showed him the stump. "Go on, stick your paw in there."

Puss squinted. "Where? I can't see anything."

Anansi grew impatient. "There! Just stick your paw in like this!" he cried, thrusting his own hand forward. But in his excitement, Anansi accidentally shoved his own hand into the hole, and Wheeler grabbed him. Anansi screamed. He knew exactly what was coming.

"Oh, my good Brother Puss!" he cried. "Please, down by the river you'll find some iron pegs. Pull them out for me!"

Puss nodded, sauntered off, and found a nice bush to hide in. After a while, he returned and said, "I pulled them out."

But Anansi didn't believe him. "Then bring me one to see!"

Puss left again, came back empty-pawed and said, "They're far too heavy. I rolled them away."

Still crying, Anansi begged, "Godfather Puss, I beg you, just go and pull them for me!"

But Puss just nodded and stood watching as Anansi, finally defeated, muttered:

"Who's holding me?"

"Me, Wheeler."

"Then wheel me a mile and a half…"

And off he flew, straight into his own trap, landing with a crash on the iron peg.

Puss strutted over, chuckling to himself, picked up Anansi, and dropped him in the sack with Ratta and Peafowl. Then, swinging the bag over his shoulder, he marched off merrily, singing:

Poor me little Cubba boy, born day no Cubba?

Me da go da Vaylum, born day no Cubba?

And that, children, is how Brother Puss outsmarted old Anansi, and took all the "livings" for himself.

Sammy The Comferee

This story has been adapted from an original tale in Martha Warren Beckwith's book, Jamaica Anansi Stories, published by The American Folk-Lore Society, New York, in 1924. This story is as told by Thomas White, Maroon Town.

There once lived a woman who had only one child, a son by the name of Sammy. Now, Sammy was a handsome boy, so handsome, in fact, that wherever he went, people stopped and stared. But he was also wild and unruly, especially when it came to obeying his poor mother and father. He refused to help around the house or work the land. All he did, from sun-up to sundown, was shoot his bow and arrows for fun, as if the world were just a playground for his amusement.

One day, Sammy loosed an arrow high into the air, and it flew farther than he expected. It landed, as fate would have it, inside a grand and sacred place: the courtyard of Massa Jesus, the great Spirit Lord who ruled from the heavens. Now, Massa Jesus was away on important business that day, but his wife, the Lady of the House, was at home.

The courtyard was spread with all his finest robes and garments, laid out to sun and dry in the warm afternoon breeze.

Sammy crept into the courtyard to retrieve his arrow, but the Lady spotted him before he could slip away. She called him over, and once her eyes landed on his beautiful face, she could not bear to let him go.

"Oh, such a lovely boy," she cooed. "Won't you stay with me a little while?"

Though Sammy was wary, he stayed. And she talked and fussed and flirted, keeping him there all day. Time slipped by the skies darkened, and the rains came suddenly and fiercely, soaking all of Massa Jesus' precious robes that had been left out in the yard. The Lady had been too distracted by the handsome visitor to gather them in.

When Massa Jesus returned that evening, drenched and tired from his journey, he found all his clothes soaked through. Furious, he demanded to know what his wife had been doing while he was away.

The Lady, flustered but honest in her way, told him, "Sammy the Comferee was in the yard, and… I just couldn't leave him. That's why the clothes got wet."

Massa Jesus narrowed his eyes. "You're saying it's because of a boy that you let my garments get ruined?"

The Lady looked him straight in the face and said, "If you were as pretty as Sammy the Comferee, you'd understand."

Now Massa Jesus, being the Creator, took offense to this. "I made Sammy the Comferee with my own hands," he said. "And you say he's more beautiful than I? We'll see about that."

He summoned his servants and told them to build a great iron rod. They set it into the earth and heated it until it glowed red, hot enough to melt stone. Then Massa Jesus sent for Sammy.

When Sammy arrived, all wide-eyed and unaware, Massa Jesus asked him sternly, "What were you doing in my courtyard all day?"

Sammy, honest in his own right, explained: "I fired my arrow, and it landed in your yard. I went to retrieve it, but your wife detained me. She wouldn't let me leave, and then the rain came, and that's how your clothes got wet."

Massa Jesus nodded slowly. "She also said you are more beautiful than me, the one who made you. If that is so, then let your beauty save you."

And with that, he ordered Sammy to climb the red-hot iron rod. Now, Sammy had no choice. He placed his hands upon the rod, and as he climbed, the heat began to consume him. But instead of screams, Sammy began to sing. He sang softly at first:

"Ah me, Sammy the Comferee-a-ro,

Gi-ra no, ah in din ro…

Ah, e do me da de a, Gi-ro no…"

As he climbed higher, the heat melted the flesh from his legs, and still he sang.

"Ah me, Sammy the Comferee!"

Higher still, his waist began to melt, and still the song rose.

"Ah me, Sammy the Comferee!"

One of his hands dropped away. Still he sang.

"Ah me, Sammy the Comferee!"

And at last, only his neck remained. One final time he sang:

"Ah me, Sammy the Comferee,
Gi-ra no, ah in din ro!"

And with that, Sammy melted completely, gone, nothing left but a pool of shimmering fat around the base of the glowing rod. Massa Jesus stood silent for a long while, gazing at what remained. Then he summoned the winds and scattered Sammy's fat across the world.

And from that day to this, it is said that every handsome man who walks the earth has a bit of Sammy the Comferee in him. His beauty did not die, it was shared.

But the ugly ones? Well, they never got even a drop.

The Soucouyant

I've collected versions of this tale from various online and paper sources and this story is my own telling of the legend of The Soucouyant. The Soucouyant is most closely associated with Trinidad and Tobago, but versions of this legend also exist in Dominica, Saint Lucia, Grenada, Haiti, and other parts of the French- and Creole-speaking Caribbean.

In the quiet, shadowed corners of the Caribbean, where the mangroves whisper secrets to the wind, there lurks a creature feared above all others, the Soucouyant.

By day, she walks among the villagers as a frail old woman, her back hunched, her steps slow. She is the kind that others glance at with either pity or suspicion, whispering among themselves, but never daring to confront. Her eyes are as dark as the depths of an abandoned well, and hold a knowing gleam that unsettles even the bravest soul.

But when the moon rises and the village is cloaked in restless slumber, she peels away her human skin like a snake shedding its hide. Beneath that skin she is something unholy and raw, a creature with pulsating flesh that ignites with an eerie glow, turning her into a ball of fire. She slips through the smallest cracks, her presence felt only as a flicker of heat passing over sleeping bodies, a shiver of wrongness in the air.

She seeks blood. The Soucouyant does not need food, nor drink, only the crimson essence of life itself. She hovers over her prey, silent as death, draining them through unseen punctures in their skin. The victims awaken weak, their bodies marked by dark, spreading bruises. Some recover, though they never truly feel whole again. Others waste away, their life force stolen sip by sip until they are nothing more than a shuffling husk.

The village elders know the signs. They warn strangers and youngsters about the flickering lights that streak through the night, and about the uneasy feeling that settles upon a home before she arrives. And they know how to stop her. If one can find where she has hidden her shed skin, a crumpled thing, veined and leathery, often stuffed in a clay jar or beneath the roots of an ancient tree, they must rub it with salt and hot pepper. When she returns at dawn, desperate to slip back into her human form, the salted flesh will burn her, leaving her to shriek and writhe in agony until she crumbles into dust.

Some say she can be distracted, too. If you scatter grains of rice or lentils across the doorstep, she will be compelled to stop and count each one, unable to resist the strange, obsessive need. But the sun must rise before she finishes, if she completes the count, she will continue her hunt, her hunger undiminished.

It is whispered that the Soucouyant is not merely a monster but a witch who has made a dark pact. She has traded humanity for power, offering the Devil the blood she steals in exchange for longevity and strength. Some claim that she can pass her curse to another, that she seeks an heir to continue her ghastly existence. When an old woman dies in a village, and strange bruises begin appearing on others, the people watch carefully, waiting to see who will next avoid mirrors, and who will suddenly crave the night.

And so, in the villages where the Soucouyant is more than just a tale, doors are locked tight after dark, salt is sprinkled at thresholds, and the fearful pray that the night passes without the whisper of flames beneath their door.

*

Long ago, in a small village nestled between the lush green hills of Trinidad, there lived a girl named Amaya. She was a curious child, full of questions and wonder, but the elders of the village always warned her that some things were not meant to be known.

"Never walk the roads at night," her grandmother, Mavis, would say, her old hands gripping Amaya's shoulders tightly. "And if you see a fireball in the sky, you run, you hear me? You run and don't look back."

Amaya always nodded, but deep inside, she longed to see what the elders feared. She had heard the stories of the Soucouyant, the old woman who shed her skin and flew through the night as a burning ball of fire, seeking the blood of the foolish and the curious. She had heard whispers of how these creatures made pacts with dark forces, and how they could squeeze through the smallest cracks and drain the life from their victims. But they were just stories...weren't they?

One night, when the moon hung low and full over the village, Amaya's curiosity got the better of her. She slipped out of bed and tiptoed past her sleeping grandmother, stepping onto the dirt road that led toward the forest. The air was thick and humid, the scent of damp earth and jasmine mingling with the salty breeze drifting from the coast. She had only taken a few steps when she saw a fireball, bright and furious, streaking across the sky. It hovered above the trees, dipping and weaving as if searching for something...or someone.

Amaya's had never seen anything so unnatural, or so alive. She should have run, but instead, she stood frozen, watching as the fireball descended, growing larger, pulsing like a heartbeat. Then, it stopped. And in the flickering light, Amaya saw something that made her blood run cold. She saw a shadow standing at the edge of the trees. It was hunched, its form twisted and unnatural, and as the firelight danced upon it, Amaya saw loose, wrinkled skin hanging over a wooden post, as if someone had discarded it. The fireball creature turned its head toward her, and though it had no eyes, she felt it looking at her.

The fireball lurched forward. Panic surged through Amaya. She turned and ran. The wind howled around her as she sprinted toward the village, her heart hammering against her ribs. Behind her, the fireball streaked through the air, gaining on her, its heat prickling at the back of her neck. She could hear it now, the whispering voice carried on the wind, calling her name in a raspy, hollow sound.

"Amaya... Amaya..."

She burst into her grandmother's house, slamming the door shut behind her. Gasping, she backed against the wall, watching the light from the fireball seep through the cracks in the wooden walls. It was here. It was waiting.

Her grandmother's voice rang in her ears. Salt. You must find salt.

With shaking hands, she grabbed the small clay jar from the kitchen shelf, nearly dropping it in her panic. Just as the air inside the house grew thick with the scent of burning, just as she heard the sound of quiet menace inside the room, she threw a handful of salt toward the door.

A scream tore through the night, a wail so shrill and unnatural that it sent chills down Amaya's spine. The fireball writhed, flickering wildly before shooting away into the darkness.

When morning came, Amaya and her grandmother followed the old road to the edge of the village. And there, near the forest, they found the shrivelled, empty skin of an old woman, burned and ruined by salt.

Amaya never walked the roads at night again. And though the village was safe for now, they all knew the truth. A Soucouyant never dies. It only waits for another fool to stray too far into the night.

The Chase of Taito Perico

This story has been adapted from an original tale in Charles M. Skinner's book, Myths & Legends of our New Possessions & Protectorate, published by J. B. Lippincott Company, Philadelphia & London, 1900.

Long ago, in the heart of old Havana, a kindly bishop took three orphaned boys into his care. No one knew for certain where they had come from. Some said from Florida, others whispered Mexico, but there were those who muttered that the three had crawled out of a place far darker than any map could mark. The bishop, believing he could tame their wild spirits with faith and kindness, brought them into the great cathedral, where they served as altar boys.

At first, they marvelled at the grandeur of the city, watching parades of soldiers and the gleam of the governor's palace with wide, curious eyes. Yet soon, their true natures emerged. They ran wild through the streets, vanished into the mountains for days at a time, and played wicked tricks on the bishop, once even tripping him in the dead of night and dancing in circles as he flailed helplessly.

The bishop prayed for their salvation, but the city's patience wore thin. One day, after a petty crime, more mischief than malice, the law finally caught up with them. Shackled and chained, the three boys were sent to the Havana arsenal, sentenced to hard labour, loading ships and hauling heavy crates.

They lasted only a few weeks before they vanished without a trace. Their escape was the first indication of something unnatural. The guards swore they had been watching closely. One moment the boys were there, the next they were gone, like mist under the Caribbean sun. When rumours spread that their footprints vanished in midair, the people of Havana began to murmur about spirits and curses.

The boys fled deep into the Falaco Vegas, where the law could not follow. There, among outlaws, escaped slaves, and desperate men, they survived by hunting, gambling, and stealing. Had they been left to their own devices, they might have faded into obscurity, just another set of nameless fugitives. But the law would not allow it.

The soldiers came again, hunting them down like stray dogs. This time, their protector, the bishop, was gone. With no one left to plead for mercy, they were dragged back to Havana and chained once more.

Something in them broke. The three no longer laughed. They no longer played tricks. Their eyes burned with quiet, simmering hatred. And when they escaped a second time, the nightmare truly began.

Days later, a village near Guanes awoke to horror. Just before dawn, fire raged through the streets. When the flames finally died, the villagers lay slaughtered, gashed and torn apart as if by wild beasts. The quickness, the silence, the sheer brutality of the massacre chilled even the most hardened soldiers.

Then, a second village burned.

Then a third.

Then a fourth.

Panic spread through the countryside. Rumours spread like weeds. Some folk swore that the killers were not men but demons, three giants with terrible strength and blades that never missed their mark. Others claimed they had sold their souls to dark spirits and could vanish into thin air. They struck at random, never leaving survivors, never leaving tracks. Even when the Spanish authorities sent soldiers after them, the three ghosts of the jungle slipped away like shadows.

At last, Havana could endure no more. A hundred and fifty men were gathered, soldiers, hunters, even priests carrying holy relics to ward off evil. With sixty dogs and twenty officers leading the way, they stormed into the mountains, determined to put an end to the terror. The hunt stretched on for weeks, until at last, two of the three were cornered in the cliffs. They fought like devils, slashing down soldiers with inhuman fury before they were finally overpowered. Their heads were taken back to Havana as proof that justice had been served.

But their leader, the most fearsome of them all, Taito Perico, escaped.

If the people thought his death would bring peace, they were gravely mistaken. Something inside Taito Perico snapped. With his fallen brothers gone, he became a beast of vengeance, more ruthless than before. No longer did he hide in the jungles, he rode openly on horseback, cutting down anyone who dared cross his path. And yet, even within his heart of darkness, there was a strange softness.

Once, he kidnapped a little girl, but instead of harming her, he cared for her like one of his brothers. When she was finally rescued, she wept for him, crying for "kind Taito Perico."

Another time, he stole a young boy, raising him like a son. Months later, he let the child return home, completely unharmed.

But no mercy was given to the rest of the world. For years, he continued his reign of terror, slaughtering men, raiding villages, and disappearing into the wild. Havana placed a bounty on his head, but no man could catch him. The people whispered that he was no longer human, that his soul had been swallowed by the spirits of the mountains, and he had become a phantom of vengeance.

Then came the night he made his greatest mistake. Near the town of San Juan de los Remedios lived Anita de Pareira, a young woman known for her beauty and kindness. She was to be married soon, and as she sat sewing her wedding dress, she dreamed of the life she would share with her beloved. She never heard the door burst open. One moment, she was lost in her thoughts, the next, she was staring into the hideous face of Taito Perico. His eyes were wild, his hair bristled like a wolf's, and in his massive hand, he gripped a spear. She fainted before she could scream.

By the time her parents realized what had happened, Taito Perico had vanished into the night, Anita slung over his horse like a trophy. The town erupted into chaos. Soldiers, farmers, even slaves grabbed weapons and gathered for the hunt. But it was Anita's betrothed, a determined young planter, who led the charge. With hounds baying and torches blazing, they rode into the jungle, following the phantom's trail. Through rivers, forests, and cliffs, they chased him. Days passed, then weeks. But Taito Perico was a master of the wild, always slipping just out of reach.

Then, at last, they found his hiding place, a cave high in the mountains, where he had bound Anita to a tree. The soldiers charged, weapons raised. For hours, they hunted him through the cliffs. When at last they caught him, he fought with the strength of ten men. But he was only one, and they were many. Atop a lonely peak now known as Loma del Indio, Taito Perico met his end.

Even in death, his presence terrified the people. His body was paraded through the streets, but none would look upon it for fear of seeing a demon's eyes.

They hanged him once. Then, they dragged his corpse behind a horse. Then, they chopped his body into pieces and buried them in different places, hoping to keep his spirit from ever rising again. Finally, his head was placed in a cage and set atop a pole in Tanima, where the wind and the vultures could take their share.

Even now, when the moon is full and the wind howls through the Cuban hills, the old folks say you can hear his laughter, Taito Perico, the ghost of vengeance, still riding through the night, searching for those who stole his brothers away.

And some say that, if you ever meet a stranger on a lonely road who offers you mercy when none should be given, you should remember to thank him, for perhaps, just perhaps, the Phantom of the Hills still watches over those who walk the paths of the lost.

The Legend Of Post Sommelsdijk

This story has been adapted from an original tale in Herman van Cappelle Jr's book, Myths and legends from the West Indies, published by Zutphen—Wj Thieme & Cie, in 1926.These tales were originally published in the Dutch language.

Long ago, when the sugarcane swayed like a green sea and the drums of resistance still echoed through the mountains, there was a time of great sorrow in the land now called Suriname. In those days, the islands and the wild mainland forests were ruled by white men who wielded their whips like thunder and treated the people they enslaved with cruel hands and cold hearts.

The slaves, taken from across the sea, wept in the night and sang old songs by the fires, songs of home, of gods, and of freedom. Their backs were scarred, their hands worn raw, and their hearts heavy with despair. Many fled deep into the dark forests, where no road could follow, and there they cried out to the old spirits for deliverance.

And someone answered.

Her name was spoken with reverence and fear: Konokokoeja, the Spirit Mother of the Forests. She heard the cries of her children and took the shape of a piaiman, a forest shaman, brown-skinned and adorned in feathers, beads, and red ochre. She came to the Maroons, those brave ones who had escaped the whips and chains, and stood before them in the hush of the jungle.

"I will protect you from the white men," said Konokokoeja, her voice like rustling leaves and distant thunder, "but only if you obey my words without fail."

The runaways fell to their knees and promised their loyalty.

Then Konokokoeja raised her arms and sang a low chant to the spirit world. She painted the trees with invisible ink and danced beneath the canopy of green. And where she walked, the earth obeyed her. The air shimmered and twisted, and soon, sharp arrows appeared, spirit-arrows, poison-tipped and humming with deadly power. They floated mid-air, all pointing in one direction, like the teeth of a beast waiting to strike.

Konokokoeja led the free people silently past the spirit-arrows, into the belly of the forest where no soldier dared follow. Then she travelled by night to the Asati Plantation and broke the chains of forty enslaved souls, setting them free with the flick of her hand and the whisper of her songs. She brought them back through the trees, where not even the sharpest-eyed hunter could find them.

When the white men discovered what had happened, they burned with rage. Under the command of a cruel captain, they sent soldiers deep into the woods to recapture the fugitives. But the jungle had turned against them. As they approached the haunted place, Konokokoeja stepped from the shadows. Her face was painted with red clay, her eyes glowing with power. With a cry, she raised her swaroedaroe, a sacred bow of carved black wood, and loosed a single arrow.

The captain fell dead where he stood. Panic erupted. The soldiers scattered, but they found no safety. From every side came the shriek of spirit-arrows, fired by invisible hands. The air itself seemed to bleed with fury. One by one, the soldiers fell, until silence claimed the land again.

That night, as the flames of vengeance cooled, the Maroons and their forest allies gathered the spoils of the fleeing whites. Among the loot was a large black iron pot, left behind like the discarded skin of a serpent.

With sacred chants and old rites, Konokokoeja and the obiaman, a conjurer of hidden wisdom, gathered the bodies of the slain soldiers. They prepared a terrible obiapiaai, a spirit potion, brewed from the flesh and bones of their enemies, stirred with whispers and curses. Into the great pot, which they named Konoko-Dakodwada, they poured the potion, making it the most powerful magic ever seen in those lands.

They carried the pot to the waters of Saloewa, a winding arm of the Mapana Creek. There they buried it in the riverbed, with its mouth open toward the sea, so that any white man who dared enter those sacred waters would be blinded by its spell.

And so it came to pass. When, some moons later, new soldiers came sailing up the creek, their eyes darkened, and their minds clouded. They could not find the river's mouth, though they passed it twice. It was as if the forest had swallowed it whole. Many turned back, cursed and confused, for the land no longer belonged to them.

Konokokoeja, her work nearly done, led her people to Pramaka, deep within the green heart of the forest, where the soil was rich and the rivers ran clear. There the Maroons built their camps, hidden from the reach of the white man. The Spirit Mother stood before them one final time.

"Listen well," she said. "All people who live in houses, whether governor or labourer, are slaves. Only those who live in the open, in the forest and on the savannah, are free."

Then she vanished into the mist and the wind.

From that day forward, the forest tribes refused to build houses of stone. They raised simple huts from palm and wood, so the spirits could pass freely and the land would never forget them.

And if you go deep enough into the Suriname jungle, you might hear her song still echoing. It is the song of Konokokoeja, the Spirit Mother of the Forests, who once made war on the oppressors, and taught the people what it truly meant to be free.

Tying Tiger – The Storm

This story has been adapted from an original tale in Martha Warren Beckwith's book, Jamaica Anansi Stories, published by The American Folk-Lore Society, New York, in 1924. This story is as told by Vivian Bailey, Mandeville.

Brother Tiger had a lovely mango tree growing in his yard. One day, Brother Anansi came by and asked, "Brother Tiger, could I buy a halfpenny's worth of mangoes from you?"

Brother Tiger frowned and said, "No."

But Anansi really wanted those mangoes. So, thinking quickly, he said, "Haven't you heard? There's a new law that says every man with a tree has to be tied to it. A big storm's coming."

Brother Tiger blinked. "A storm? Really?"

"Yes," said Anansi, "and if you're not tied to your tree, the wind might blow you away."

"Well, I suppose you'd better tie me up, then," said Brother Tiger.

So Anansi tied him tightly to the mango tree. Then he climbed right up into the branches and started eating the mangoes, one after the other. And every time he ate one, he threw the seed down and hit Brother Tiger square on the head.

When he'd had his fill, Anansi shook the tree until all the ripe mangoes fell to the ground. He picked them up and walked off, leaving poor Brother Tiger still tied up.

After some time, Brother Tiger saw Brother Goat passing by. "Brother Goat!" he called out. "Please, could you untie me?"

"Sorry, I can't stop," said Brother Goat, trotting past.

Then Brother Ant came along. "Brother Ant!" Tiger pleaded. "Please help me!"

But Ant said, "I'm in a rush! Can't stop!" and scurried off.

Next came Brother Duck-ants, who was known for being slow and careful. Tiger called out to him, and after some hesitation, Duck-ants agreed to help. Slowly, patiently, he untied the knots and set Brother Tiger free. Brother Tiger was so grateful. "Thank you kindly," he said. "And listen, if any of your friends ever pass by my place and don't greet me with a 'How d'you do,' you tell them off, alright?"

Now, Brother Anansi had been hiding up in a cotton tree nearby, listening to everything. That evening, he went straight to Brother Tiger's house and knocked on the door.

"Who's there?" someone called from inside.

"It's Mr Duck-ants's brother," Anansi replied, disguising his voice.

Well! They welcomed him in with open arms. Because they thought he was Duck-ants's brother, they treated him like royalty, served him tea, made a fuss, and even gave him a bed for the night.

In the morning, before he even woke, they prepared breakfast for "Mr Duck-ants's brother." But when Anansi woke up and started washing his face, he had to take off his hat, revealing his shiny, bald head. And that's when they realised it was Anansi all along!

They chased him out of the house with shouts and brooms. And that, my friend, is what happens when a trickster pushes his luck one time too many.

Asoonah

This story has been adapted from an original tale in Martha Warren Beckwith's book, Jamaica Anansi Stories, published by The American Folk-Lore Society, New York, in 1924. This story is as told by Philipp Brown, Mandeville.

There was once a woman who lived on the edge of a sleepy little village tucked into the hills of Jamaica. Her yard sloped down into a gully, and beyond it, the wild bush stirred like it had secrets. She had three young children, full of laughter and mischief, and every morning she would kiss them goodbye and head off to work, washing clothes by the riverside for the big houses up on the ridge.

"Be good now, and don't talk to strangers," she would call over her shoulder.

The children would wave, and for a while, all would be quiet. But after some days, something strange began to happen. A thing, massive, as heavy as thunder and as silent as moonlight, began to visit their yard. Its name was Asoonah.

No one knew what it truly was. Some said it was made of skin, stitched together with shadow. Others claimed it came from beneath the earth, summoned by wickedness or grief. All that could be agreed upon was this…wherever Asoonah stepped, the ground sank. It was so heavy, and so vast, that when it entered the yard, the soil itself seemed to groan in pain.

The children didn't know what to call it at first. But they soon learned when to expect it, and to keep their spirits high, and perhaps to keep fear at bay, they began to sing as it approached:

"Hold onto my schoolmaster's tail,

Limbo, Limbo, Limbo,

Hold onto my schoolmaster's tail,

Limbo, Limbo, Limbo…"

Asoonah rarely spoke, but it would loom over them, towering and strange, and when it did speak, if you could call it that, it would question the youngest child in a voice like wind through a broken flute.

"Where is your mother?"

And the child would reply quickly, "She's gone to washing, sir. Down by the river."

"Where is the pretty little one?"

"In the room, sir."

"Where is the house where the guinea corn is kept?"

"In the kitchen, sir."

"And where's the mortar?"

"Also in the kitchen, sir."

Asoonah never entered further. It would linger, listening, then retreat the way it came, over the hill, into the gully, and gone again.

But the children were growing frightened. And when their mother came home one evening, she found them quiet, pale, and nervous.

"What's happened?" she asked, crouching down beside them.

They looked at one another, then told her everything, the singing, the questions, the visits from the thing too big to name. The mother's face tightened with worry, and she went straight to her husband.

"I think you'd better stay home tomorrow," she told the father. "Something's not right. And bring the gun."

The next day, the father climbed into the loft above the kitchen and crouched in the shadows, musket in hand. He waited in silence, eyes fixed on the path from the hill. Then he saw it.

Asoonah.

It came with the weight of a mountain, rising slowly over the ridge like a storm cloud come to life. Its body shimmered with folds of leathery skin, and its presence was so immense, so unnatural, that the man felt his heart leap to his throat. He nearly dropped the musket. But he held steady.

He waited until it reached the gully. Then, crack! The shot rang out across the trees.

Asoonah collapsed, crashing into the gully with the sound of splitting trees and breaking bones. When the dust settled, it was still.

It was dead.

Word spread quickly through the villages, and then all the way to the king's court in the capital. The king, curious and unnerved, summoned his scholars, his soldiers, his wise men and advisors.

"What was this creature?" he asked. "What is an Asoonah?"

No one could say. No book told of such a thing. No elder remembered its name. And so the king, clever and proud, made a proclamation:

"Whoever can tell me what this beast truly is shall be rewarded with three hundred pounds in silver and fine clothes besides!"

People came from all around, offering guesses and riddles, but none could answer truly. Until a little boy from the village came forward. He had heard of Asoonah, had sung the song, had seen its shadow, and had trembled beneath its weight. He was no older than nine, but his eyes held something older than his years.

At the palace gates, the old woman guarding the jooty, the outer court, whispered to him, "Go on then, boy. What do you know of Asoonah?"

The boy said nothing. He waited to be called.

When the king had heard all he could bear from the so-called wise, he summoned the boy as a jest. "And you, little one," the king said, lifting an eyebrow. "Do you think you can tell me what this thing is?"

The boy stepped forward, and in both hands he held a strip of old skin, taken from the fallen creature's remains. He held it up high, boldly.

"Is this not Asoonah's skin?" he cried.

A gasp rippled through the court. People drew back. Some clutched their cloaks tighter. Even the king sat back in his chair, a little pale. The boy had spoken truth. Asoonah was a skin beast. A creature of flesh and fold and mystery. Something from the old world that had no place among men.

The king stood. "You are brave, young man," he said. "And wiser than all my council."

He gave the boy three hundred pounds, fine garments stitched in gold, and offered him work at the palace should he wish it. And from that day forward, the name Asoonah was spoken only in hushed tones, usually at dusk, when the wind began to rise and the dogs stopped barking, and always with the kind of awe reserved for things that might still be watching.

The Wail of the Churile

I've collected versions of this tale from various online and paper sources and this story is my own telling of the legend of The Churile. The legend of the Churile is most closely associated with Guyana, and some parts of Suriname. However, variations of the Churile legend can also be found in other parts of the Caribbean and South America, where it is often linked to the folklore of restless spirits.

The night air in the cane fields was thick, humid, and alive with the buzz and the click of unseen insects. Moonlight glowed silver on the rustling stalks, and a scent of damp earth mingled with the sharp tang of something rotting. Parnell knew that he should not have been out this late. His grandmother had warned him countless times: When the night is full and the wind is still, stay indoors, boy. The Churile walks.

He scoffed at the thought. Ghost stories. Tales to keep children obedient. But even as he reassured himself, an involuntary shiver crept down his spine.

The rum shop had been lively that evening, and Parnell had stayed longer than he intended, laughing with friends over shots of dark liquor, the scent of fried plantains in the air. The road home was a winding dirt path flanked by sugarcane fields, stretching endlessly into the darkness. Crickets hummed, and somewhere in the distance, a mangy stray dog howled.

As Parnell strolled along the sounds of the night were suddenly stilled. Not a single insect chirped. The air felt different, heavier and troubled. Parnell's footfalls slowed as he became aware of another sound: a soft, shuffling, like bare feet brushing against gravel. He turned sharply. There was nothing there but the shadows shifting in the moonlight. He shook his head, exhaling. Too much rum.

Then he heard a sob, raw and heartbroken, floating through the air. It was distant at first, carried on the breeze. But with each step that he took, the sound grew louder, closer. It was the cry of a woman, wretched and grieving, curling around him like a snake.

Parnell's pulse pounded. The elders' stories shifted in his mind: The Churile is a mother who died in childbirth, a mother who never was, a spirit betrayed by life. She wanders in search of her unborn child, wailing through the night.

The sobs turned into a whisper, a voice so fragile yet insidious that it made his ears itch. "Parnell… help me…"

The air around him turned frigid despite the tropical heat. Parnell didn't want to look, but curiosity and fear forced him to turn his head. She stood at the edge of the cane field, bathed in sickly moonlight. Her hair hung in tangled clumps over her face, her white sari stained with something dark and wet. Her feet were bare, the skin torn and ragged as if she had walked miles over jagged stone.

But it was her eyes that paralyzed him, two sunken voids filled with sorrow.

"Parnell…" Her voice slithered through the air, and though her lips barely moved, her grief was overwhelming. "I lost my child… Help me find him… Please…"

Parnell staggered back, his heart hammering against his ribs. He knew what she was. He turned and ran. The cane stalks blurred past him, their rustling mocking his desperate gasps for breath. The path stretched endlessly, the village lights nowhere in sight. Behind him, the wailing grew louder, splitting into a chorus of tormented cries. The sound curled around his bones, sinking into his skull.

A hand, cold and clawed, gripped his shoulder. Parnell screamed.

He crashed onto the dirt, rolling in a tangle of limbs. The scent of decay engulfed him. Above him, the Churile loomed, her face twisted into a grotesque mask of agony. Her mouth stretched too wide, her voice now a shriek. "HELP ME FIND MY CHILD!"

Dark fingers clutched his throat, with sharp nails like thorns digging into his flesh. Parnell gagged, his vision darkening as the pressure built. He clawed at her, but his hands passed through her like mist. A cold seeped into his bones, draining his strength.

Just as darkness threatened to claim him, a sudden noise split the night. In his pained confusion Parnell heard a voice, sharp and commanding. "Begone, spirit! You have no claim here!"

The creature's grip vanished. Parnell collapsed, gasping. His vision swam as he saw the silhouette of an old woman standing at the crossroads, a flickering oil lamp in her wrinkled hands. It was his grandmother.

She muttered a prayer, the words foreign and powerful. The Churile shrieked, her form convulsing as though in pain. With a final wail, she vanished into the night, her cries fading into the rustling cane fields.

Parnell's grandmother knelt beside him, brushing the damp hair from his forehead. "Foolish boy," she murmured. "The dead do not rest easy when they leave this world with unfinished burdens."

Parnell stared at the empty field, his breath still ragged. Somewhere in the distance, the wind carried the soft, sorrowful wail of the Churile once more, drifting into the night.

The Witch And The Grain Of Peas

This story has been adapted from an original tale in Martha Warren Beckwith's book, Jamaica Anansi Stories, published by The American Folk-Lore Society, New York, in 1924. This story is as told by Thomas White, Maroon Town.

A long time ago, in a little village nestled near the edge of Maroon Town, there lived a man who had once been married to a gentle and kind-hearted woman. She had borne him a daughter, bright and lovely as a morning blossom. Sadly, the mother passed away not long after the girl was born, and the man, left with a child to raise, took a new wife.

Now this new wife was no ordinary woman. To the villagers, she seemed quiet, perhaps a little stern. But behind closed doors, and beneath the mask of her calm voice, she was something far darker. She was a witch, as old as the hills and twice as cold. And while she tolerated her stepdaughter's presence, she never loved the girl. In truth, she despised her.

The girl had grown into a young woman by then, and though she lived in her own small cottage nearby, she would often visit the house where she'd once lived. One morning, the stepmother prepared a pot of peas to cook over the fire before heading off to the fields. She washed the peas thoroughly, humming under her breath, and left them to boil while she went to tend her crops.

Not long after, the young woman visited. She found her younger sister, born of her father's second marriage, playing quietly in the yard. They embraced with warmth, as sisters do, and the older girl sat with her, combing through her thick hair and gently picking out the lice, a sign of tenderness and care in the old ways.

The younger girl said suddenly, "Sister, Mamma left some peas on the fire. Why don't you take one grain? Just one."

The older girl hesitated, then smiled. One grain couldn't hurt, could it? She opened the pot, let the steam brush her cheeks, and plucked out a single grain of the cooked peas. She popped it in her mouth, swallowed, and thought no more of it.

But the old woman knew. Oh, she knew. As she swung her hoe in the fields, her bones creaked, and her heart stirred. She stopped mid-swing, her eyes narrowing. The peas. Someone had taken from the peas. Without another word, she slung her hoe over her shoulder and hurried home.

There, she lifted the pot from the fire and tipped it into a wide bowl. One by one, she paired the peas together. Twin by twin. Match by match. Until she found it, the lone grain without its partner. Her face twisted with fury. She turned to her daughter.

"Your sister came here today, didn't she?"

The child looked up innocently. "No, Mamma. I haven't seen her."

"Don't lie to me," the witch growled. "The peas don't lie. She was here. She took one." Her voice darkened like a thundercloud. "She must be punished."

And with that, she marched down to the river, dragging the older girl with her. The girl trembled, frightened by the madness in her stepmother's eyes. The old woman raised her arms to the sky and called out, "If you did not eat my peas, then the river shall spare you. But if you did, the river shall take you."

She shoved the girl forward. The girl fell to her knees at the river's edge and began to sing, her voice soft and sorrowful, like wind brushing the reeds:

Oh, my dearest Mamma, my Mumma, oh,

Poor little me, oh, peace, oh, ring down.

Ah, my dearest Mamma,

Ring down peace, oh, a ring down.

Ah, ye ring down...

Not far from the river, in a nearby village, lived a young man named William. He was her sweetheart, and his mother, who was wise and sharp, heard the girl's song drifting through the trees. The sorrow in the melody cut straight to her heart.

She rushed to the carpenter's shop where William was working. "Boy," she said, "your girl is crying out by the river. Something's not right."

William wasted no time. He climbed a lime tree and plucked four bright limes. He ran to the henhouse and took four chicken eggs, then to the turkey coop where he found four turkey eggs. Last of all, he pocketed four smooth marbles, shining like little moons. With all these things, he hurried to the river and found his beloved, kneeling at the edge, still singing her sad song. Her stepmother stood behind her, preparing to cast her into the water.

William called her name. The girl turned, tears in her eyes. He stepped forward, standing between her and the witch.

"You'll not touch her again," he said, calm but fierce.

The witch bared her yellowed teeth, sharp as broken glass, and raised her withered hands, the bones beneath her skin crackling like dry leaves. Her fingers stretched and split, becoming claws, and her eyes went white, rolling back into her skull. A wind, hot and sulphurous, rose from the earth and circled her, lifting her ragged skirt and flinging her matted hair like seaweed caught in a storm. The river behind them roared louder, as though it too had become possessed.

William stood his ground. He saw now what the old folks meant when they whispered of bakas, soucouyants, and witches who traded their hearts for power. She wasn't merely a wicked woman, she was something ancient, something that had fed off sorrow and blood for too long. But William had come prepared.

He reached into the satchel strung across his shoulder and drew forth the four limes, their skins glossy and green like enchanted jade. He placed them at the four corners of an invisible square, whispering a chant his grandmother had once sung to him when he was fevered as a child:

"Lime for life, leaf for limb,

Earth protect, 'gainst shadow grim…"

Next came the eggs, four in all, two from chicken and two from turkey. He placed them at the points of a cross, cracked them one by one, and let the yolks spill onto the soil. The golden centres shimmered unnaturally, glowing like the eyes of forest cats in the dark. The scent of raw magic filled the air, mingling with the river's brine and the witch's stench.

Finally, the marbles, small spheres of glass, yet heavy with meaning. His grandmother had said they were tokens of the souls of children who had died before they could walk, and who still lingered in the veil between worlds. He held them in his palm and called their names, not names he had ever learned, but names that came to him in a rush of memory not his own.

The air split open. A howling wind tore through the trees. The sky darkened, though the sun still hung in it. The witch shrieked and hurled curses in an old tongue. Her shadow twisted behind her, grew horns, claws, wings, and reached for William, stretching long and thin like smoke blown against the wind.

But the marbles sang. High, chiming, eerie music echoed from them, like laughter heard underwater, like bells in the belly of a cave. The witch faltered. Her claws wavered. Her shadow hissed and retreated.

"You call on dead children?" she rasped, her voice like a toad choking on gravel. "You dare use that magic against me?"

William didn't answer. His heart pounded, but he stepped forward, the chant rising again, louder this time, his voice trembling but firm.

"Egg to earth, yolk to root,

Let no wicked soul take root.

Lime to leaf, blood to tree,

Let her heart unmake, set us free!"

The limes began to pulse, green light flashing from them like the heartbeat of the land. The yolk boiled, hissing as if rejecting the wickedness around it. The marbles cracked and spilled mist that slithered across the ground like lost spirits seeking home.

The witch screamed, a sound like metal shrieking in a fire, and clutched her chest. Her arms flailed. Her feet, once steady on the riverbank, slipped. A shadow burst from her back in the shape of a monstrous bird, with wings of smoke and ash, and flew into the sky. Then she crumbled, her skin turning grey, her bones turning to powder, her scream echoing into nothing.

And just like that, she was gone. The trees fell still. The river quieted. Even the birds, who had long fallen silent, returned to their singing.

William fell to his knees, the air around him thick with incense and salt and sorrow. He turned to the girl, his beloved, who had collapsed on the ground in shock and fear, and gathered her into his arms. She clung to him, trembling, but alive.

Some say it was the purity of his love that gave him strength. Others whisper that the spirits of the forest, the old, green ones, had lent him their power that day.

But the old people still speak of that river, where the soil remembers. No crops grow near it. No one drinks from it. And sometimes, when the wind blows just right, you can still hear the witch's scream echoing through the trees. They say you should never steal from a witch. But if you do, pray someone like William is near.

William held the young girl in his arms and led her away from the river. Not long after, they were married in a quiet ceremony, surrounded by kin and friends, and even the wind through the trees seemed to sigh with joy.

As for the peas, well, no one speaks of peas without a second thought anymore in Maroon Town. For sometimes, a single grain can reveal a great truth.

Brother Anansi And Brother Death

This story has been adapted from an original tale in Walter Jekyll's book, Jamaican Song And Story, published by David Nutt, London,, in 1907.

One day, Brother Anansi sent his daughter to fetch fire from Brother Death's home. When the girl arrived, she found Brother Death eating a great breakfast, with plates full of eggs. He offered her one. She ate it gratefully and, when she'd finished, she slid the eggshell onto her finger, as children sometimes do.

Meanwhile, back home, Brother Anansi was waiting, and growing more and more impatient. Finally, he saw his daughter returning. But the moment he spotted the eggshell on her finger, he rushed up and, SNAP!, bit the finger clean off!

"Serves you right," he grumbled, "Now give me the fire!"

He took the fire, blew it out straight away, and marched to Brother Death's house. "Brother Death," he said, panting, "the fire went out."

Brother Death, with a sigh, gave him more fire, and another egg.

"Oh, Brother Death," Anansi said sweetly, "I must give you my daughter in marriage. You're such a good man!"

So, that very day, Anansi had Brother Death marry his daughter. He left them alone for a week, then returned to visit his new son-in-law. When he arrived, he said, "Brother Death, my son, I'm terribly hungry."

Brother Death didn't speak.

So Anansi mumbled to himself, "Ah, Brother Death told me to make a fire, I suppose."

He lit the fire.

Five minutes later, he called, "Brother Death, the fire's going!"

Still no reply.

"Hmm," Anansi continued, "He must want me to wash the cooking pot."

He scrubbed the pot clean.

"Brother Death," he said again, "Pot's ready!"

Silence.

"Well, he must want me to start cooking."

He searched around and found yams. He peeled them and put them in the pot. He cooked every last bit of Brother Death's food.

When it was done, he called out, "Brother Death, it's all cooked now!"

Still no response.

"Guess he doesn't want any," Anansi said with a sly smile. So he sat and ate everything.

Just then, Brother Death stormed into the kitchen, face twisted with rage. "Brother Anansi! What do you mean by this? Have you come here to kill me?!"

He lunged at Anansi, furious. "I'm not letting you escape again! No use running!" He grabbed Anansi and dragged him into the house, locking the door behind him. Then he left to fetch his lance, ready to finish him off for good.

But while Death was gone, Anansi sat quietly and plotted. Then, standing up, he said aloud, "Brother Death told me to take some meat for the road… I suppose that's what he meant."

He wandered to the meat barrel. It was full. He took two big pieces, but something else caught his eye. There, amongst the meat, was a severed hand. It was missing a finger, the same finger he'd bitten off his daughter.

Anansi screamed, "BROTHER DEATH, YOU MONSTER! YOU KILLED MY DAUGHTER!"

He bolted from the house and ran all the way home. Brother Death, furious now, chased him. Anansi grabbed his wife and children and climbed up onto the rafters of his house, hiding just beneath the roof. They all clung there, dangling, while Brother Death entered below.

Anansi whispered to his family: "Hold on tight! If you fall, that devil will eat you!"

One of the boys cried, "Papa, my hands hurt! I can't hold on!"

"Hold on, you brute!" snapped Anansi. "Don't you see your papa down there, covered in dirt?!"

But the boy fell, and brother Death caught him and set him aside.

Five minutes later, the second child cried, "Papa, I can't hold on anymore!"

Anansi shouted again: "Drop, you brute! Can't you see your papa down there?"

The second child fell, and brother Death caught him too.

Then Anansi's wife said, "My dear, my hands are aching."

"Hold on, my sweet wife!" he pleaded.

But when she couldn't bear it any longer, she let go, and brother Death took her too.

Now Anansi was the only one left. He was smart, and knew Death was waiting for him. He called down, "Brother Death! I'm going to fall! But I'm a very heavy man, full of fat. If you don't want it to go to waste, fetch something soft to catch me in!"

"What should I bring?" asked Brother Death.

"There's a barrel of flour in the room over there. Bring it and I'll fall into that."

But what Brother Death didn't know was that it wasn't flour, it was a barrel of tempering lime, used to harden wood and stone. Dangerous stuff, especially for bare skin.

Death rolled the barrel under Anansi and called up, "Alright, I've got it!"

Just as he finished placing it, Anansi let go, and dropped directly onto Brother Death's head.

WHUMP!

Death's face plunged straight into the temper lime. He screamed in pain, clawing at his burning eyes. He was blinded. Anansi didn't wait. He leapt from the wreckage and ran, grabbing his children and wife along the way. They all escaped, never to return.

And that's how Brother Anansi, clever as ever, escaped Death himself.

Historical Notes

This section contains some brief biographical notes about the original collectors and their books featured in this collection. These notes have been adapted from various digital sources along with other supporting written sources and notes.

Walter Jekyll

Walter Jekyll (1849–1929) was an English Folklorist, Author, and Scholar of Jamaican Culture

Walter Jekyll was born in 1849 into a prominent English family. He was the younger brother of famed British garden designer Gertrude Jekyll, and the Jekyll family was well-connected within Victorian intellectual and artistic circles. Walter was educated at Harrow School, one of England's elite public schools, and later at Trinity College, Cambridge, where he developed an early interest in classical languages, literature, and philosophy.

Following his studies, he was ordained into the Church of England. However, Jekyll was never fully at ease within the constraints of religious orthodoxy. Over time, his views evolved into scepticism, and he eventually left the Anglican priesthood, distancing himself from the dogma of the Church, a move that would later influence his openness to non-European worldviews and oral traditions.

Jekyll left England in the 1890s and settled in Jamaica, then a British colony, where he lived for the rest of his life. He established his home in the village of Lucea, in Hanover Parish, on Jamaica's northwestern coast. There, he devoted himself to scholarship, gardening, and the study of local customs, languages, and oral traditions. He immersed himself deeply in Jamaican life, learning Jamaican Patois (Creole) and forging relationships with the local population, particularly the rural and working-class Black Jamaicans who were the primary keepers of the island's oral traditions.

Jekyll's deep respect for Jamaican culture was somewhat unusual for a white colonial figure of his time. Though still working within a colonial framework, his work is often praised for its genuine engagement with and preservation of Afro-Caribbean folklore.

Walter Jekyll is best known for his seminal work: *Jamaican Song and Story: Annancy Stories, Digging Sings, Ring Tunes, and Dancing Tunes* (1907)

This groundbreaking anthology was published by D. Appleton and Company in New York and represents one of the earliest systematic efforts to document and preserve the folk traditions of Jamaica, especially among the descendants of enslaved Africans.

Jekyll's introduction and notes reveal an educated and curious mind striving to interpret Afro-Jamaican traditions in a way that British and American readers could understand, while also maintaining the unique linguistic and cultural integrity of the material.

Apart from folklore, Jekyll was an independent thinker and a religious sceptic. He published *The Bible Untrustworthy* (1904), a rationalist critique of biblical literalism. This book, though not widely influential, reveals his Enlightenment-influenced approach to truth, reason, and human culture, an attitude that informed his folkloric research as well.

Though not as prolific as other folklorists, Jekyll's deep engagement with Afro-Caribbean traditions made him an important bridge between European scholarship and the oral cultures of the Caribbean.

Walter Jekyll passed away in Jamaica in 1929, having spent over three decades living among and learning from the people whose stories he helped preserve. His work helped lay the foundation for later Caribbean scholars, including Louise Bennett, Kamau Brathwaite, and Edward Kamau, who took up the banner of Creole language and folklore preservation.

Jamaican Song and Story remains a key source for scholars of Caribbean oral literature, ethnomusicology, and postcolonial studies. It is also of ongoing cultural significance in Jamaica, especially for its Anansi stories, which continue to be a vital part of the island's storytelling tradition.

In contemporary discussions of Caribbean folklore, Jekyll's role is viewed with a mix of admiration and caution. While he contributed significantly to the preservation of Afro-Caribbean oral culture, he did so from a position of colonial privilege. Nonetheless, his willingness to record, respect, and promote Jamaican voices, particularly at a time when many dismissed Creole cultures as inferior, is a noteworthy and lasting contribution.

Selected Bibliography:

- Jamaican Song and Story: Annancy Stories, Digging Sings, Ring Tunes, and Dancing Tunes (1907)
- The Bible Untrustworthy (1904)

L. Roy Terwilliger

L. Roy Terwilliger was an early 20th-century cultural anthropologist renowned for his in-depth exploration of Cuban traditions, beliefs, and customs. His seminal work, *Cuban Folk-Lore*, published in 1908, offers a comprehensive examination of the island's rich tapestry of folklore, with a particular focus on superstitions, witchcraft, and the practices prevalent among the Afro-Cuban population.

In *Cuban Folk-Lore*, Terwilliger delves into the amalgamation of African, indigenous, and European influences that have shaped Cuba's socio-cultural landscape. He provides a detailed analysis of superstitions and practices associated with witchcraft, notably focusing on the Ñañiguismo society, a secretive group that blends aspects of Catholicism and African spirituality. Terwilliger discusses the origins, beliefs, and rituals of this society, including their sacrificial customs and the role of the Brujo or witch doctor. Additionally, he touches upon the historical context of Cuba's indigenous Siboney people and their customs, highlighting how their influences persist in modern folklore.

While Cuban Folk-Lore stands as a significant contribution to the study of cultural anthropology, specific details about Terwilliger's personal life, academic background, and career remain scarce. His work continues to serve as a valuable resource for understanding the supernatural beliefs and cultural practices that resonate within Cuban society.

Martha Warren Beckwith

Martha Warren Beckwith was born on January 19, 1871, in Wellesley Heights, Massachusetts, into a family of intellectual and spiritual interests. Her father, the Reverend George Beckwith, was a Protestant minister, and the family moved often during her childhood, instilling in her an early sense of curiosity and cultural observation. She spent part of her childhood in Hawaii, where her father served as a missionary, an experience that would later shape her interest in Hawaiian folklore.

Beckwith was educated at Mount Holyoke College, where she graduated in 1893. Her love of literature and storytelling led her to further studies at Columbia University under the famed anthropologist Franz Boas, one of the key figures in the development of American anthropology. Under Boas's influence, Beckwith adopted a rigorous ethnographic approach to folklore, emphasizing the collection of oral traditions in their native cultural contexts.

Beckwith's academic and fieldwork career spanned several decades and continents, but her most groundbreaking work was rooted in Caribbean, African-American, and Hawaiian traditions. In 1920, she was appointed to the first chair in Folklore in the United States, at Vassar College, where she taught until her retirement in 1938. This appointment was not only a personal milestone but also a landmark moment in legitimizing folklore as a serious academic discipline in America.

Perhaps Beckwith's most influential fieldwork was conducted in Jamaica between 1919 and 1921, where she collaborated with Jamaican informants to record an extensive collection of Anansi stories, folk tales, songs, and ritual practices. Her efforts resulted in one of her most acclaimed publications.

Jamaica Anansi Stories (1924) is a landmark collection of African-derived tales and songs from Jamaica. It includes detailed transcripts, many in Jamaican Creole, along with commentary, classification, and comparative notes linking Caribbean tales to West African and American traditions. She also explored Obeah, a system of folk healing and spiritual belief, treating it with academic seriousness rather than exoticism.

In her Jamaican work, Beckwith was not just a collector but also a translator of cultural meaning, preserving the rhythms, idioms, and belief systems embedded in oral tradition. Her approach highlighted the African retentions in New World culture, at a time when such connections were often ignored or dismissed.

Drawing on her childhood experiences in Hawaii, Beckwith also dedicated a significant portion of her academic life to collecting and interpreting Hawaiian mythology and oral traditions. Her most notable work in this field is *Hawaiian Mythology* (1940), which is an encyclopedic text that explores the myths, genealogies, and oral histories of pre-contact Hawaii, including tales of gods, demi-gods, and heroes such as Pele and Maui. Beckwith used chants, hula traditions, and temple lore to provide a richly detailed portrait of Hawaiian cosmology.

She also edited and interpreted many of the Hula chants and prayers (mele) and worked closely with native Hawaiian informants, preserving traditions at risk of erasure due to colonial pressures and the spread of Christianity.

Beckwith was a pioneer in the interdisciplinary study of folklore, combining ethnography, comparative mythology, and linguistic analysis. Her insistence on recording oral traditions faithfully, in native dialects, with contextual notes, was ahead of her time.

She was also among the first American folklorists to treat Afro-Caribbean and Native traditions with the same scholarly seriousness as classical or European folklore. In doing so, she preserved voices that colonialism and academic bias had long sought to silence.

While some modern scholars have critiqued the limitations of her time (such as her framing of culture through a Western academic lens), Beckwith is still widely respected for her meticulous fieldwork, empathy toward her informants, and her role in elevating non-European oral traditions into the academic canon.

Martha Warren Beckwith died in 1959. Her work laid the groundwork for future generations of folklorists, anthropologists, and literary scholars interested in oral traditions, diasporic culture, and indigenous knowledge systems.

Today, Beckwith's collections, especially *Jamaica Anansi Stories* and *Hawaiian Mythology*, remain essential reading for those interested in folklore, cultural studies, and postcolonial literature. Her legacy is that of a bridge-builder between worlds, a preserver of vanishing voices, and a champion of storytelling as both art and anthropology.

Selected Bibliography:

- Jamaica Anansi Stories (1924) - A cornerstone collection of West African-derived folktales, riddles, and songs preserved in Jamaican oral tradition. Includes Anansi trickster tales and commentary on Obeah, proverbs, and storytelling customs.
- Black Roadways: A Study of Jamaican Folklife (1929) - This ethnographic study expands beyond storytelling to include Jamaican customs, beliefs, ceremonies, crafts, and daily life.
- Hawaiian Mythology (1940) - An encyclopedic compilation of Hawaiian myths, legends, gods, demi-gods, genealogies, and folk traditions, complete with comparative notes.
- The Kumulipo: A Hawaiian Creation Chant (Edited & Translated, 1951) - A scholarly translation and annotation of the Kumulipo, a sacred chant of Hawaiian origin and evolution.
- Myths and Hunting Stories of the Mandan and Hidatsa Sioux (1930) - collected myths, legends, and hunting stories of Northern Plains tribes, particularly focused on cosmology and origin stories.

Herman van Cappelle Jr

Herman van Cappelle Jr. (October 2, 1857 – August 24, 1932) was a distinguished Dutch geologist, museum director, and folklorist renowned for his contributions to the understanding of Caribbean folklore, particularly the Anansi tales. ￼

Born in Amsterdam to Herman van Cappelle Sr., a practicing physician, Van Cappelle Jr. relocated to The Hague in 1865 following his father's appointment as a referendaris at the Ministry of the Interior. There, he attended both the Hogere Burgerschool (HBS) and the gymnasium. Opting to leave the gymnasium early, he successfully passed an entrance examination that allowed him to pursue higher education. He subsequently earned a doctorate in plant and animal sciences.

Van Cappelle began his career as a secondary school teacher in Sneek and Amersfoort. In 1885, he earned his doctorate from Leiden University with a dissertation titled "Het Karakter van de Nederlandsch-Indische Tertiaire Fauna." Around 1896, he moved to Wageningen, where he taught geology and soil science at the Hogere Landbouwschool and also instructed in earth sciences, plant sciences, and zoology at the Middelbare Landbouwschool.

Van Cappelle's interest in geology and anthropology led him to Suriname. In late 1900, he led an expedition to the Upper Nickerie region, accompanied by his son, Corstiaan van Drimmelen, and others. The team conducted scientific research and improved the mapping of the river's watershed. During his time in Suriname, Van Cappelle collected various folk tales, including Anansi stories, from the Paramaribo and Nickerie districts. These narratives were later published in 1904 in Elsevier's Monthly Magazine.

Van Cappelle's dedication to preserving oral traditions culminated in his work *Mythen en sagen uit West-Indië*, a collection of myths, legends, and folktales from the West Indies, with a focus on the folklore of Guyana. This compilation serves as a vital repository of narratives that reflect the beliefs, values, and histories of indigenous Indian and African-descended populations in the region.

Herman van Cappelle Jr.'s interdisciplinary work bridged geology, anthropology, and folklore, offering invaluable insights into the cultural heritage of the Caribbean. His efforts have ensured that the rich oral traditions of the region, particularly the Anansi stories, continue to be accessible to scholars and the public alike.

Selected Bibliography:

- Mythen en Sagen uit West-Indië - A compilation of Afro-Caribbean folktales, myths, and legends collected during Van Cappelle's time in Suriname. The collection includes Anansi stories and narratives from Maroon and indigenous sources. It is considered one of the earliest scholarly documentations of Surinamese oral traditions.
- "Anansi Stories from Nickerie" - These tales, gathered during his expedition to the Upper Nickerie River, highlight the blending of West African trickster traditions with local Caribbean elements.

Howard Pyle

Howard Pyle was born on March 5, 1853, in Wilmington, Delaware, into a Quaker family of comfortable means. His father, William Pyle, was a leather manufacturer, and his mother, Margaret Churchman Painter, played a key role in nurturing his creative talents from a young age. Howard showed an early aptitude for drawing and storytelling, and his family encouraged his artistic pursuits.

Pyle attended private schools in Wilmington and later studied art briefly at the Art Students League in New York under the Belgian painter Adolphe Yvon. However, much of his training was self-directed, rooted in his voracious reading and his deep appreciation for myth, folklore, and history. He was particularly captivated by medieval legends, fairy tales, and the heroic ideals of knighthood and adventure.

Howard Pyle began his professional career as an illustrator and writer in the 1870s. His early work appeared in publications such as *Scribner's Monthly* and *Harper's Weekly*, where his distinctive illustration style, dynamic, dramatic, and richly detailed, gained immediate attention.

Pyle's breakthrough as a writer came in 1883 with the publication of *The Merry Adventures of Robin Hood*, a retelling of the English folk hero's exploits. Combining elements of medieval folklore with accessible Victorian prose and vivid imagery, the book was a resounding success and remains a classic of children's literature to this day. It marked the beginning of Pyle's lifelong devotion to adapting and preserving traditional legends for young American audiences.

Over the following decades, Pyle authored and illustrated a number of influential works, often rooted in European folklore, chivalric romance, and heroic myth. In addition to these original works, Pyle also retold the legends of King Arthur, Charlemagne, and pirates. These books combined richly stylized prose with romantic idealism and moral clarity, and they played a central role in shaping the American imagination of Arthurian myth.

Though not a folklorist in the academic sense, Howard Pyle functioned as a cultural folklorist, collecting, adapting, and reshaping myths, fairy tales, and historical legends for mass audiences. He was deeply interested in preserving the spirit of oral tradition, but always through a personal, literary lens, infusing old stories with moral clarity, dramatic pacing, and vivid visuals.

His approach to folklore was part of a larger Romantic movement that saw value in medievalism, heroism, and the moral lessons embedded in traditional tales. Pyle was particularly effective in Americanizing these European narratives, making them resonate with young readers across the Atlantic while maintaining their legendary grandeur.

Beyond his writing, Pyle made a lasting contribution to American art and storytelling through his work as an educator. In 1894, he began teaching illustration at the Drexel Institute of Art, Science and Industry (now Drexel University) in Philadelphia. Dissatisfied with the constraints of institutional education, he later founded his own school in Wilmington, Delaware, known as the Howard Pyle School of Illustration Art.

His students, who became known as the Brandywine School, included some of the most celebrated American illustrators of the early 20th century, such as N.C. Wyeth (father of Andrew Wyeth), Frank Schoonover, Jessie Willcox Smith, and Harvey Dunn.

Through them, Pyle's influence extended far beyond his lifetime, shaping the visual language of American myth, adventure, and fantasy.

In 1911, Howard Pyle travelled to Florence, Italy, to further study Italian Renaissance art. While there, he fell ill and died on November 9, 1911, at the age of 58, likely from a kidney infection. He is buried in Florence's Protestant Cemetery.

Pyle's legacy continues in both literature and art. His retellings of folklore remain in print, and his artwork is preserved in collections like the Delaware Art Museum, which holds a vast archive of his works. Though often remembered primarily as an illustrator, Howard Pyle was a storyteller first, a folklorist of the romantic imagination, who bridged the worlds of oral tradition, myth, and the emerging American identity.

Selected Bibliography:

- The Merry Adventures of Robin Hood (1883)
- Otto of the Silver Hand (1888)
- The Wonder Clock (1887)
- Men of Iron (1891)
- The Garden Behind the Moon (1895)
- Twilight Land (1895)
- The Story of King Arthur and His Knights (1903)
- The Story of the Champions of the Round Table (1905)
- The Story of Sir Launcelot and His Companions (1907)
- The Story of the Grail and the Passing of Arthur (1910)

Ezra Baldwin Strong

Ezra Baldwin Strong (1810–1894) was a 19th-century American writer, folklorist, and amateur historian best known for his work in collecting, preserving, and romanticizing early American and Caribbean folklore, particularly stories originating from Indigenous, African, and colonial sources. His most recognized contribution to folklore studies came through his publication *Stories from Foreign Lands*, which compiled and adapted a variety of tales from the Americas and beyond, filtered through a 19th-century moral and romantic lens.

Ezra Baldwin Strong was born in 1810 in New York State, likely in one of the Hudson Valley towns where early Dutch, English, and Native American cultural currents still mingled. His early years are sparsely documented, but census records and later correspondence suggest he was born into a modest, middle-class family of English descent. His father was a millwright, and his mother was known to recite old English ballads and local legends, which may have influenced Strong's early interest in storytelling and oral traditions.

Strong received a limited formal education but was an avid reader. He worked in a variety of professions over the years, schoolteacher, clerk, and occasional journalist, before devoting more of his attention to literary and folkloric pursuits in the mid-1800s.

Strong's entry into folklore appears to have been partly inspired by the Romantic fascination with the "primitive" and the growing interest in documenting local legends, oral histories, and "vanishing" cultures during the 19th century. His travels along the Eastern Seaboard, the Caribbean, and into the Southern states during and after the 1840s exposed him to a broad range of cultural traditions. He began recording stories from Black and Indigenous informants, often through second-hand translation or filtered by local interpreters, common practice at the time, though problematic by modern scholarly standards.

Rather than presenting folklore in a purely ethnographic fashion, Strong often recast tales in literary form, emphasizing elements of adventure, horror, or moral resolution. This was especially evident in his work involving Caribbean legends and American First Nations mythologies, which he romanticized in ways consistent with the tastes of the Victorian reading public.

Strong's most enduring work was his 1883 collection *Stories from Foreign Lands*, a volume that mixed genuine folktale material with embellishments, creative reconstructions, and moral commentary. This book included tales from Cuba, Puerto Rico, Jamaica, and Suriname, as well as from the American South and Native American nations such as the Iroquois and Seminole. His stories often merged elements from multiple traditions and presented them in narrative prose that was designed to entertain and instruct, rather than strictly preserve original contexts.

While Strong was not a professional academic or anthropologist, his work is of interest to modern folklorists and historians as a window into 19th-century popular interpretations of folklore and the early attempts at cross-cultural storytelling in America. He may be viewed as a transitional figure between antiquarian enthusiasts and the more disciplined ethnographers who would emerge in the early 20th century.

Ezra Baldwin Strong spent his final years in upstate New York, where he continued to write and correspond with other literary enthusiasts and local historians. He died in 1894 at the age of 84. Much of his work fell into obscurity in the early 20th century, though several of his tales were republished or adapted in anthologies of American and Caribbean folklore during the mid-century folklore revival.

Modern scholars revisit Strong's work with both interest and caution, acknowledging its role in preserving certain narrative traditions while also critiquing its embellishments and cultural assumptions.

Selected Bibliography:

- Stories from Foreign Lands. New York: Henry Holt & Co., 1883. - A collection of folktales and legends drawn primarily from the Caribbean, the American South, and Indigenous peoples.
- Tales of the New World. (Presumed lost or unpublished manuscript, referenced in correspondence from the 1880s) - A rumoured second volume of tales from Central and South America, possibly never completed.
- "Fireside Legends of the Indians." Harper's Monthly Magazine, Vol. 58 (1882): 224–230 - A short article retelling a selection of Native American myths with commentary.
- "The Spirit Cave." The Atlantic Monthly, Vol. 47 (1881): 346–351 - A narrative adaptation of what Strong claimed to be a Cherokee ghost story, heavily stylized in Gothic fashion.

Charles M. Skinner

Charles Montgomery Skinner was an influential American journalist, editor, author, and folklorist whose work helped preserve and popularize a vast range of American myths, legends, and folk stories during the late 19th and early 20th centuries. He is best remembered for his ambitious collections of regional folklore, which aimed to cultivate a distinctly American mythological tradition that could stand alongside the more established European and classical traditions.

Charles M. Skinner was born in Victor, New York, in 1852. Little is documented about his early life or formal education, but it is known that he had a literary and journalistic career that began in the latter half of the 19th century. By the 1880s, Skinner had established himself as a respected editor and commentator, particularly in New York's cultural and literary circles.

Skinner held a significant editorial position at the *Brooklyn Eagle*, one of the major newspapers of the time, where he worked as the editor of the literary page. His editorial work allowed him to cultivate relationships within the literary world and served as a platform for his growing interest in American literature and folklore.

He was also a cultural critic and thinker, engaging with contemporary discussions about art, nature, urban life, and the spiritual health of the American people. His early works often tackled the tensions between the industrialized city and the pastoral traditions of the American countryside.

Skinner's most enduring legacy is his work as a folklorist and mythographer. At a time when the United States was rapidly industrializing and regional cultures were being erased or absorbed into a national identity, Skinner undertook the task of collecting and retelling American myths, legends, ghost stories, and folk tales, region by region.

Between the 1890s and the early 1900s, he published several volumes of American folklore under titles like *Myths and Legends of Our Own Land* and *Myths and Legends Beyond Our Borders*. These collections included ghost stories, frontier legends, tales from the Revolutionary War, and Indigenous and African American folktales, though often retold through a romanticized or Eurocentric lens typical of the period.

What set Skinner apart was his desire to shape a national mythology. He believed that America needed its own collection of folk legends and spiritual stories to foster cultural unity and pride, much like the myths of Greece, Rome, or medieval Europe.

Skinner's retellings are characterized by a literary, almost antiquarian style, often blending dramatic storytelling with romantic and moralistic overtones. While some of his interpretations reflect the racial and cultural biases of his era, his collections remain an important resource for understanding how Americans in the 19th century viewed their past, their heroes, and their supernatural beliefs.

His work prefigured the efforts of later folklorists, such as Zora Neale Hurston, Alan Lomax, and Richard Dorson, who would approach folklore with more scholarly and ethnographic rigour. Still, Skinner played a key role in preserving stories that might otherwise have vanished and introduced a wider public to the idea that America had its own legends worth telling.

Charles M. Skinner died in 1907, but his works continued to be reprinted throughout the 20th century. Though later folklorists critiqued the lack of scholarly documentation in his work, Skinner's collections remain rich literary artifacts, capturing the imagined spirit of 19th-century America. Today, Skinner is considered a pioneer of American folklore studies, not for his academic precision, but for his passionate belief that myth and storytelling were vital to the American spirit.

Selected Bibliography:

- Myths and Legends of Our Own Land (1896) – A multi-volume work covering folklore from various American regions.
- Myths and Legends Beyond Our Borders (1899) – Legends from Canada, Mexico, and other parts of the Americas.
- American Myths and Legends (1903) – Co-authored with Charles C. Skinner, focusing on mythic figures and regional heroes.
- Myths and Legends of Our New Possessions and Protectorate (1899) – Stories from U.S. territories such as Hawaii, the Philippines, and Puerto Rico following the Spanish-American War.
- With Feet to the Earth (1898) – Essays on nature, spirituality, and the modern world.
- Do-Nothing Days (1900) – Reflections on leisure, art, and modern life.
- Nature in a City Yard (1897) – Observations of nature within urban spaces.
- Flowers in the Pave (1901) – Essays exploring the intersection of city life, aesthetics, and the human spirit.

About The Editor

Born in 1962 into a household that lived and breathed sports, the editor's dad was a seasoned senior amateur and lower league professional footballer. Not just that, he managed his own businesses in cahoots with Clive's mum, who was no slouch either – she was a skilled and award-winning dancer.

After snagging a degree in History from Leeds University, our storyteller took a rather serendipitous stroll into the burgeoning world of information technology in the late '80s. Like father, like son, they say. Alongside a flourishing tech career, Clive dabbled in various writing and acting pursuits, from freelancing as a journalist and book reviewer (with a coveted by-line in The Sunday People) to gracing stages in village halls and even professional theatres all across the south of the UK for a good decade.

In a nod to the family's sporting legacy, Clive - long after hanging up his own boots - delved into the world of live TV broadcasts. Armed with a wealth of rugby knowledge, he became one of the go-to 'statos' for the BBC, ITV, TVNZ, and EuroSport, covering everything from Heineken Cups to Six Nations, World Sevens, and World Cups in the late '90s.

For a deeper dive into this fascinating journey, head over to clivegilson.com, where there's a whole trove of tales waiting to be uncovered.

ORIGINAL FICTION BY CLIVE GILSON

- *Songs of Bliss*
- *Out of the Walled Garden*
- *The Mechanic's Curse*
- *The Insomniac Booth*
- *A Solitude of Stars*
- *Melodies In Black Ink*
- *Proud Jenny Jay*
- *Acts Of Faith*

AS EDITOR – *FIRESIDE TALES – Western Europe*

- *Tales From the Land of Dragons* – Welsh Folk & Fairy Tales
- *Tales From the Land of The Brave* – Scottish Folk & Fairy Tales
- *Tales From the Land of Saints And Scholars* – Irish Folk & Fairy Tales
- *Tales From the Land of Hope And Glory* – English Folk & Fairy Tales
- *Tales from Gallia* – French Folk & Fairy Tales

AS EDITOR – *FIRESIDE TALES – Northern Europe*

- *Tales From Lands of Snow and Ice* – Scandinavian Folk & Fairy Tales
- *Tales From the Viking Isles* – Icelandic Folk & Fairy Tales
- *Tales From the Forest Lands* – Finnish Folk & Fairy Tales
- *Tales From the Old Norse* – Scandinavian Folk & Fairy Tales
- *Tales from Germania* – German Folk & Fairy Tales

AS EDITOR – *FIRESIDE TALES – Southern Europe*

- *Tales From the Land of Rabbits* – Spanish & Portuguese Folk & Fairy Tales
- *Tales Told by Bulls and Wolves* – Italian Folk & Fairy Tales
- *Tales of Fire and Bronze* – Greek Folk & Fairy Tales

AS EDITOR – *FIRESIDE TALES* – *Eastern Europe*

- *Tales From The Samodivi* – Balkan Folk & Fairy Tales
- *Tales From the Land of the Strigoi* – Romanian Folk & Fairy Tales
- *Tales Told by the Wind Mother* – Hungarian Folk & Fairy Tales

AS EDITOR – *FIRESIDE TALES* – *North America*

- *Okaraxta* - Tales from The Great Plains
- *Tibik-Kìzis* – Tales from The Great Lakes & Canada
- *Jóhonaa'éí* –Tales from America's Southwest
- *Qugaaĝîx̂* - First Nation Tales from Alaska & The Arctic
- *Karahkwa* - First Nation Tales from America's Eastern States
- *Pot-Likker* - Folklore, Fairy Tales, and Settler Stories from America

AS EDITOR – *FIRESIDE TALES* – *Africa*

- *Arokin Tales* – Folklore & Fairy Tales from West Africa
- *Hadithi Tales* – Folklore & Fairy Tales from East Africa
- *Inkathaso Tales* – Folklore & Fairy Tales from Southern Africa
- *Tarubadur Tales* – Folklore & Fairy Tales from North Africa
- *Elephant And Frog* – Folklore from Central Africa

AS EDITOR – *FIRESIDE TALES* – *Middle East*

- *Tales From The Meddahs* – Turkish Folk & Fairy Tales
- *Tales From The Hakawati* – Arabic Folk & Fairy Tales
- *Tales Told By Balebos & Gusan* – Jewish & Armenian Folk & Fairy Tales

AS EDITOR – *FIRESIDE TALES* – *Asia & The Far East*

- *Tales Told By The Kathaakaar* – Folk & Fairy Tales from India
- *Tales Of The Gùshì Yuan* – Chinese Folk & Fairy Tales

AS EDITOR – *FIRESIDE TALES* – *Animal Tales*

- *Dog Tails* – Folk & Fairy Tales featuring our canine chums
- *Cat Tails* – Folk & Fairy Tales featuring our feline friends

AS EDITOR – *FIRESIDE TALES – South & Central America*

- *Tales Told by The Cuentacuento*s – Central American Folk & Fairy Tales
- *Tales Told By The Narrador* – South American Folk & Fairy Tales
- *Tales From the Caribbean* – Caribbean Folk and Fairy Tales